KNIGHTS OF THE
SQUARE TABLE 2
— DEAR WORLD —

KNIGHTS OF THE SQUARE TABLE 2
— DEAR WORLD —

Teri Kanefield

Armon
Books
San Francisco

Armon
Books
San Francisco
945 Taraval Street, #130
San Francisco, CA 94116

Summary: Empowered by their experiences while stranded on an island, six teenagers set out to right the wrongs in the world. When unconventional—and illegal—methods get them into trouble, they find themselves on the run.

A story of hope and adventure.

List of Characters Introduced in Book 1 and Book 1 Plot Summary

The **Knights of the Square Table**, San Francisco's ninth-grade all-star chess team, includes the following six members:

Alexis has a take-charge attitude and often stands with her arms akimbo. She likes hiking, being outdoors, and arguing. She thinks of herself as tough. Really, she has a kind heart and likes to defend people who need protection.

Cindy is calm, introspective, and shy with strangers. She has a photographic memory. She loves to collect things: photographs, books, old maps, knickknacks. She is very observant and good at sizing people up.

George is the team captain. He is a natural politician and speaks with a compelling authority. His family assumes one day he'll be president of the United States. George is fluent in three languages.

Liam thinks of himself as the ultimate geek. He likes music and poetry. He plays several instruments, but favors the saxophone. He had a lonely early childhood as an only child with parents who worked long hours.

Natalie, a peacemaker by nature, is the most easygoing and agreeable member of the group. In fact, she is so sweet and gentle, with no rough edges at all, that she doesn't even seem like the type to be on a chess team. It's only after you get to know her that you realize how smart she is. She is pretty and petite.

Spider's real name is Michael, but nobody except his parents calls him that. Spider got his nickname because he likes to climb. He climbs mountains, rocks, anything at all. He's strong with a wiry build and long spindly legs and arms that do, indeed, make you think of a spider. He likes making jokes. He is the most playful member of the group.

Don, the pilot, was flying the plane from Germany to the United States when the avionics system failed and he had to make an emergency landing on a remote island in the North Atlantic. He's a nice, easygoing guy who developed a deep respect for the Knights of the Square Table while they were stranded together on the island.

Veronica, one of the passengers on the plane, is a thief, a troubled woman with a troubled background, who describes herself as a "psycho."

Mars is the name the Knights of the Square Table

gave the island where they were stranded.

The president of the Democratic Republic came to power when a revolution created a new country in Asia.

Plot Summary of Book 1: The Knights of the Square Table gain confidence while stranded on an island when their resourcefulness and ingenuity help all the passengers survive. After they are rescued, they feel empowered and confident enough to take on the task of solving a missile crisis.

When they successfully avert a nuclear war, Cindy believes the group is capable of solving other major problems in the world.

A question that sometimes drives me hazy:
am I or are the others crazy?
—Albert Einstein

1

Alexis chose prison reform as her topic, and she was already sorry. She chose it because of a research project she'd done in her criminal justice elective, and because she'd always assumed one day she'd be a lawyer. Her parents, anyway, had been saying she was going to be a lawyer since she was four years old— the age she first started arguing with everything. Her sister was fond of saying that Alexis didn't care which side of the argument she was on, as long as there was an argument and she was in it.

Reading about prisons in America was not a fun way to spend a Saturday. She imagined that Spider, whose issue was saving the environment from destruction, had already abandoned his reading and headed for a hiking trail. She admired his sense of fun. She wished she, too, could just toss off all worries the way he did.

Now, after their success in averting a war, Cindy genuinely thought they could solve the major problems in the world, and where to start but with research? So they listed what they believed were the six greatest problems in the world, and divided them up.

Alexis had gone along with Cindy's idea. She didn't *always* want to be the person saying, *come on, guys, no way.*

Reading about prisons made Alexis think of Veronica, so, curious, she googled her name. Veronica's last name, Hollick, was unusual enough that not much came up, except a court listing showing that two days earlier, she'd been arrested for violating Penal Code sections 484 and 459.5.

Aw, geez, she thought. She reached for her phone and found the phone number for Veronica's aunt. It was easy to locate, being the only incoming call she'd ever received from the 916 area code. When Veronica's aunt answered, she said, "Hi, it's Alexis, Veronica's friend from the airplane."

"Of course! I talked to you a few weeks ago. You're the cute blonde kid with the ponytail who helped Veronica on the island."

Alexis bristled. *Cute blonde kid?* She was not used to hearing herself described in diminutives. Okay, she wore her hair in a ponytail, but that was only because she hadn't bothered to cut it and ponytails were easier. She did not think of herself as cute.

"So Veronica got arrested?" Alexis asked.

"Yup. She's in jail in Sacramento. I was heading up there this morning to visit her. I'll tell her you called."

It wasn't hard to guess what had happened. "She stole something else," Alexis said, dismayed.

"Sometimes I think she has a secret death wish or something. It's like she *wants* to go to prison."

Alexis nodded to herself, remembering how Veronica had wandered away from the plane and sat by herself in the snow. Something was definitely wrong with Veronica.

"What's her problem? Is she a kleptomaniac?"

"Unfortunately, it's much more complicated than that. She obviously has a problem with stealing, so kleptomania is part of it. She has other issues as well, antisocial stuff, personality issues, major depression. Don't get me started."

"Where are her parents?"

"They died when she was young. I'm not sure you want to know the gory details. Drug abuse was part of it."

"What did she steal?" Alexis asked.

"Clothes. From Macy's. Wouldn't you think she could have at least stolen clothes on sale instead of the most expensive dress and jacket on the rack? Last time she was in for five years. This time the prosecutor wants fifteen years."

"*Fifteen years?* For stealing a dress and jacket?" Alexis asked, even though, after some of the things she'd been reading lately, she wasn't surprised.

"Yup," Tammy said. "She's had a few convictions. And she doesn't say the things she's supposed to say to get leniency. It doesn't mean a judge would actually give her fifteen years, but that's what the prosecutor is asking for."

Alexis thought of Veronica spending even five

years in one of the prisons she'd read about and she felt sick to her stomach.

"I want to visit her, too," Alexis said. After reading about prisons, part of her wanted to see a jail or prison. Another part wanted to hide from it all and join Spider on the hiking trail.

"She's allowed two visits a day," Tammy said. "If you don't mind doubling up with me, I'll be able to spend longer with her."

"That's fine with me," Alexis said. "I'll talk to my parents and check the train schedules and get back to you."

They said good-bye and hung up. Alexis looked up train schedules from the Bay Area to Sacramento—it was a ninety-mile trip, less than two hours each way. Her parents were at the table in the kitchen, drinking coffee. She walked in, sat down, and explained that Veronica from the plane was in jail in Sacramento and she wanted to visit her.

"I'll take you," Alexis's father said. "I'll get a Zipcar."

Her parents didn't own a car. No need to own a car in the city, her father always said. When he or her mother needed a car, they walked over to 19th Avenue and rented a Zipcar.

"The train goes right there, Dad," Alexis said. "I can go by myself. You've got stuff to do, remember?"

"What stuff?" he said. "I'll get Edwin to fix the faucet. Repairing the sidewalk can wait."

"You're not going by yourself," her mother said.

"I'll be with Veronica's aunt Tammy!"

"I prefer to go, too," her father said.

"But why drive and pollute the air?" Alexis said. "I can sit on the train and read. I have a ton of reading to do."

"The train is not a bad idea," her father said. "We'll go on the train."

Alexis sighed and gave up. She was perfectly capable of riding the train herself to Sacramento. She'd been taking public transit around San Francisco by herself since sixth grade. But obviously her parents didn't agree.

At least she didn't have the kind of parents who would say no way, you are not visiting someone in jail. Alexis's mother said visiting the sick was a good deed. She probably figured this was almost the same.

When she called Tammy back, her father got on the phone. He and Tammy arranged the time and meeting place.

She packed her knapsack. Her electronic tablet was fully charged, loaded with all the articles she'd been planning to read. Her mom gave her a few snacks for the trip.

She and her father rode rapid transit to the train station in Richmond, where he bought two round-trip tickets to Sacramento. Once they were on the train, he got himself a decaf from the snack bar and an orange juice for her, and they sat at a table. He read the news on his tablet. She read through her articles on the prison system. He didn't ask what she was reading or why. He probably figured she was doing homework.

After a while, she had to stop reading. It was just too depressing. She powered off her tablet and put it into her bag. She turned to the window and pressed her cheek to the glass. They were zooming through the Central Valley, which meant flat terrain with farmland in all directions.

She turned and noticed a newspaper on the floor. The headline said, "Fighting breaks out on the borders of the Democratic Republic."

"Oh, geez," she said aloud. She picked up the newspaper. Someone had stepped on the newspaper with dirty shoes, so there was a footprint directly on top of the article. The words, though, were completely legible. She read the article and looked at her father.

"I was just reading about that," he said. "It looks like a group who fled during the fighting is sabotaging the peace."

"Why?" she asked, dismayed. She felt an actual pain in her chest.

"You always take these things to heart, Alexis," he said gently. "It's good that you're so caring, and disciplined, and conscientious. These are really good traits. But sometimes there's just nothing you can do about a situation."

"Yeah," she said, and turned back to the window, even though if there was ever a time she could have argued with her father and told him he was wrong, this was it. She and her friends *had* done something about the situation. Maybe in the end, it hadn't done any good—maybe things would end up right back where they were before, but at least for a while, they'd averted a world war.

She wished she could feel the pure joy the others felt over what they had done. No doubt what they did was amazing. But she seemed to be the only one who understood that they'd essentially blackmailed a world leader, and doing something like that might not turn out well in the end. Once all that food and supplies poured into the Democratic Republic, the dictator probably felt very differently about George and what they'd done, but he still wouldn't like being forced. If the word ever got out that a few teenagers had backed him into a corner, he'd be thoroughly humiliated.

They were approaching a town called Davis when she received a text message from George.

"*We're meeting at Liam's this afternoon instead of tomorrow,*" George wrote.

"*I'm on my way to Sacramento!*" she wrote back. "*To visit Veronica in jail. I won't be back until later this afternoon.*"

"*We'll be there all day,*" George responded. "*Liam's ordering pizzas. We'll probably still be there when you get back. Our official agenda is to play chess and do homework.*"

"*And the unofficial agenda is to save the world from its own mistakes,*" she wrote.

"*Exactly.*"

"*Then I'd better get my reading done.*"

2

Natalie sat next to her older sister Marissa on the Muni-49 heading toward Nob Hill. Her sister, a junior in high school, was on her way to the main library.

"All right," Marissa said. "Spill it. What's on your mind?"

"Nothing," Natalie said.

"Something is wrong. You've been distracted lately. Problems at school?"

"No," Natalie said, turning to look directly at her sister. She didn't like lying, but her sister would never understand the things on her mind. Besides, there was too much she wasn't allowed to tell. Nothing was exactly wrong at school. It was just that her classes all seemed trite, unimportant, and so *ordinary* after their time on the island and hacking into the Democratic Republic website. Natalie was beginning to share Cindy's feeling that they should be doing something bigger and more important than studying advanced ninth-grade algebra.

"Boy trouble, then?" Marissa asked.

Natalie smiled. "No."

"I mean, other than fighting off all the guys after my beautiful little sister."

"I don't have to fight anyone off," Natalie said. But then she remembered the hurt in Spider's eyes when she avoided going out somewhere with just the two of them, and she felt a pang of guilt.

She turned back to the window. Ever since that conversation with Spider, she'd been questioning herself. After all, she thoroughly enjoyed being with him, and she did like him a lot. The problem was that she didn't like him *that* way. As cliché as it sounded, she liked him as a friend. He just wasn't the type of guy she imagined herself with romantically. And she'd already made the mistake once of saying yes to a guy she didn't like that much. A few months before the Germany trip, she agreed to go for ice cream with Bryan, a neighborhood guy two years older than her, and after that he literally became obsessed with her. He called her several times each day, and took to hanging out in front of her house until she felt so uncomfortable she finally had to tell him that she didn't want to see him anymore. And that wasn't fun.

Not that she was afraid Spider would do anything like that. She just didn't want to hurt his feelings.

She also wondered if she was wrong. What if the way she felt about Spider was the way you were *supposed* to feel about a guy you went out with? Maybe enjoying someone's company, laughing at his jokes, and genuinely liking him were what it was all about. Maybe she thought there was something more to it when there wasn't.

"If you're not fighting the boys off now, you *will* be," Marissa said. "Trust me about that. Beautiful and sweet is a rare combination. You're brilliant, too, but I don't expect guys your age to appreciate that. So what's on your mind? You can tell me."

Natalie studied her sister. Natalie and all her siblings had a strong family resemblance, the same big doe-like thickly-lashed brown eyes tinged with gold, high cheekbones, a heart-shaped face, and heavy dark curly hair.

Natalie grew up adoring her older sisters, especially Marissa. As a small child, she was happiest when Marissa and Michelle—who was now in her first year of college—included her in their games. Marissa had a relaxed, easygoing manner. Of her sisters, Marissa was the one she was most comfortable confiding in. Natalie felt that she and Marissa had become closer since Michelle had moved out to attend college.

Natalie thought she might as well tell Marissa part of it. "Do you realize how many nuclear bombs there are in the world? Twenty *thousand*, that's how many."

Marissa laughed. "*That's* what's bothering you? I was afraid something was wrong at school. Or maybe home."

Natalie turned away, hurt. "It seems to me twenty thousand nuclear bombs in the world are more serious than something wrong at school or home."

"Oh, Natalie! I didn't mean to laugh at you! I just felt relieved that nothing was wrong at school. Yeah, I know about all those bombs. Depressing, right?"

"Very," Natalie said.

"I used to worry about stuff like that, too," Marissa said.

"You don't anymore?"

"It bothers me sometimes, but there's just nothing I can do. I think most people are upset when they first realize the extent of the problem—then they just get used to it."

When the bus stopped at Market Street, Marissa stood up, put her backpack on her shoulder, and said, "Have fun with your friends. Play some chess. You'll feel better."

* * *

Liam put fruit and a bowl of chips on the table. Jacy Skye's music came from the speaker. He turned the volume lower, and then he went to the window to watch.

His heart beat a little faster when he saw Natalie come round the corner. He stepped back from the window so she wouldn't see him watching. When he heard the doorbell, he pressed the buzzer mounted on the wall to let her in, then sat in a chair at the table and listened to her footsteps on the stairs.

He breathed slowly and deeply to make sure he was relaxed. The last thing he wanted was for Natalie—or anyone else for that matter—to guess that when he was near her, his pulse started racing. He needed to keep the secret not only because Spider was his buddy and everyone knew Spider was in love with Natalie, but also because if Natalie didn't know how he felt, she couldn't possibly reject him. He didn't think he would take rejection as well as Spider seemed to be taking it.

She came into the room and said, "Hi!" She looked around and said, "I'm the first one here?"

"Yup. Everyone else should be here soon. Except Alexis. She'll be late."

Natalie put her backpack on the floor and sat across the table from him.

"You did world hunger, right?" she asked. "How did *your* research go?"

"Not so good. There are organizations working on the problem. They work nonstop year after year, but never make much progress. You'd think the solution would be simple—make sure all people have sustainable food sources and make the people who have enough stop wasting—but it isn't so easy. It takes money and cooperation."

"I really don't know what Cindy thinks we can do about all these problems," Natalie said.

The doorbell rang. Liam went to the window to look. "Both George and Spider," he said, then buzzed them in.

Liam and Natalie waited in silence while George and Spider climbed the stairs. George and Spider came into the room and said hi.

From the speakers came Jacy Skye singing "How It Goes." Liam turned off the music. "Jacy was always my favorite pop artist," he said. "Now I'm not so sure anymore."

"I'm such a geek," George said, putting his

backpack under the table. "I don't even know who she is."

"She's been number one on the charts all year," Natalie told George.

"I like her music," Liam said. "But lately her lyrics have started to seem self-absorbed to me."

"Yeah," Natalie said. "I know what you mean. Mostly she writes about herself and her feelings."

"And the haters who hate her," Liam said.

Spider felt a little uncomfortable, and a little left out of the conversation. He liked Jacy Skye's music. He never thought too much about it. He liked how it sounded, and that was enough for him.

Liam pushed some buttons. Soft classical guitar came from the speakers. "How about this?" he asked.

"Very nice," Natalie said.

That was when George's phone buzzed. He picked it up and read the text. "It's from Cindy," he said. "She'll be late, too."

"Nothing much is going to happen without Cindy," Natalie said.

Liam pulled a chessboard from a shelf. "Anyone want to play?"

"I will!" Natalie said.

"Me, too," George said.

Liam put the chessboard and box of pieces on the table. Natalie and George set up their pieces. Spider and Liam leaned forward to watch.

Liam helped himself to another slice of pizza. Even Spider, whose grandfather served mouth-watering thin-crusted pizza in North Beach, admitted that this pizza was excellent. The crust was baked to perfection, the tomato sauce tangy and perfectly spiced, the cheese rich and mild.

Cindy had arrived an hour ago. They'd been debating what to do the entire time and had come up with nothing. Apparently Cindy didn't have any specific ideas. She was depending on the collective brains of the group to come up with a solution.

Now Liam thought someone needed to give everyone the truth and put an end to the whole conversation. He figured the truth-giver may as well be himself.

"Okay, everyone," he said, sitting back at his place at the table. He put his slice of pizza down on the plate in front of him and said, "Let's face the facts. It's hopeless. It was a good idea. Very ambitious. Save the world from itself. Solve the problems of the world—hunger, global warming, overcrowded prisons, and all the rest of it. But it's pretty obvious there's nothing we can do about all these problems. So we'll just have to go back to being an ordinary chess team."

"Maybe we started too big," Cindy said. "Maybe we should just concentrate on what those bank executives did when they pocketed millions of dollars in unfair fees." For months, the newspapers had been carrying stories about how the executives at the Commerce and Loan Bank had overcharged their customers millions of dollars in unfair and hidden fees. While they had to give back some of the money, they'd managed to keep millions of dollars that they'd essentially stolen.

That was when the buzzer sounded. Liam looked out the window and said, "It's Alexis." He buzzed her in.

They listened to her footsteps as she climbed the three flights. She paused in the doorway, looked them all over, and said, "Why all the sad faces?"

"Not sad," Natalie said. "We're just realizing there's nothing we can do about all the world problems. We'll just have to get used to living with twenty thousand nuclear bombs in the world."

"Yes," Liam said. "We're mourning the death of our collective innocence."

"That was very dramatic, Liam," Alexis said. She walked over to the table. She put her backpack on the floor, then sat down.

"How's Veronica?" Cindy asked.

"Bad," Alexis said. "I can tell you this. A jail is one creepy place. People are in shackles, wearing weird jumpsuits. They're treated like animals. And that was only a *county jail*. Think what a *prison* is like."

"Poor Veronica," Natalie said.

"The only thing saving Veronica right now from having one miserable life is that she has a very cool aunt Tammy. She's a hippie from the sixties. She even drives one of those hippie buses, an old VW bus. Hers is lavender with flower decals. She has two bumper stickers. One says, 'I'm already against the next war.' The other says, 'If you're not out outraged, you're not paying attention.' I think she lived in that van for a while. Now she rents a trailer with a bunch of people."

"Can she bail Veronica out?" George asked.

"Fifteen grand? No *way*. Without bail money, Veronica has to stay there until her trial. From what her aunt said, it will be a slam dunk in the guilty department. I guess she got caught red-handed."

"Too bad," George said. "But no surprise."

"If we were in charge of the world," Alexis said, "things would be run much better. Petty thieves wouldn't be put into prisons for years and years. People wouldn't starve while other people waste so much food and everything else. Look how well we did on the island."

"Yeah," Spider said. "What's up with that? Why doesn't everyone just put us in charge of the world?"

"You know," Liam said, "being on that island was like going all the way back in time before the whole world got so screwed up. You just live off the land. You don't try to take anyone else's land. You don't stupidly ruin the environment because you know if you do, you'll die. It's not like you can dump toxins in your backyard and then call for take-out Chinese food."

Cindy drew in a deep breath and said, "I know you'll all think I'm crazy, but I still think there's something we can do, at least about those bank executives keeping all that money."

Liam felt a little dismayed at that. He honestly didn't think there was anything they could do—or should do about all these world problems. They should just be happy with what they'd already done and not push their luck. Even if they spent the rest of their lives doing things like hacking into the Democratic Republic's computer system and averting nuclear disaster, they'd just have to keep doing that sort of thing over and over because people weren't going to stop doing stupid things.

Wouldn't that just get tiring? The whole Superman superhero thing worked in the movies. It made for some exciting adventures. But in real life, putting on your superhero costume and averting disaster every time one was about to happen would just wear a person out and start to feel like spinning on a merry-go-round. Eventually you'd just want to stand back and let the world destroy itself.

Besides, he still thought Cindy was a little nuts. Wasn't it a little odd for a fifteen-year-old girl to think she could solve all the world's major problems?

"What can we do about those bank executives?" George asked.

"We already decided what to do about that,"

Spider said. "We can hack into the bank, take the money they stole, and give it to the poor."

"That's not a bad idea," Cindy said.

"It's a *terrible* idea," Alexis said. "You're talking about bank robbery! Veronica is looking at fifteen years for stealing a dress from a store! We'd probably go to jail for life!"

"Nah," George said, "we're just kids."

"Sorry, but that doesn't work," Alexis said. "Want the statistics? I've been reading about it for a week now. We'd be in prison. For a long time. You can joke about being Robin Hoods, but we'd be criminals, and I can tell you that saying the ends justify the means will not fly with bank robbery."

Cindy was watching the others carefully. It was pretty clear there was nothing she could do now. If she pushed, there would be mutiny. She could see there would be no swaying Alexis. Liam was ready to abandon the whole save-the-world campaign. Natalie would never take a strong stand at this stage. They'd collectively tell her no, and then she'd be stuck. This time they'd say she was crazy, and they'd mean it. And maybe she was. That possibility occurred to her. Wasn't the plan forming in her mind the kind of idea a totally crazy person would come up with?

She knew she needed to tread gently.

4

Cindy started by emailing George articles about what happened in the courts with the Commerce and Loan Bank, also known as the C&L. Then she sent him links to the actual court documents, including rulings by the judge.

He read everything she sent him. He was a strong reader, but some of the stuff she sent was dense, with so many words he had to look up that reading the articles was slow and cumbersome. As dense as the stuff was, it was pretty clear C&L had pocketed about $30 million in unfair fees. They'd pulled a number of tricks—for example, not updating account balances on time so people thought they had money in their account when they didn't, then, when they tried to make a withdrawal, the bank charged them an outrageous fee. People would get their statements and discover that the bank had removed hundreds of dollars from their savings accounts to cover withdrawal fees. Because the people who had to pay the fees were those who didn't have extra money in the bank, the fees had mostly been collected from middle-class and lower-income customers.

In the words of one of the judges who saw the evidence, the C&L had been "gouging" its customers. One newspaper claimed the money collected from unfair fees over the years was as high as $2 billion, but it seemed to George that claim was exaggerated. Thirty million seemed like the most accurate number.

The court approved a settlement requiring the bank to return $10 million to customers. People criticized the judges for allowing the bank to keep so much of the money, but from what George understood there wasn't much more the judge could do under the law.

The part that was just plain annoying was that the bank executives had grown wealthy over the past decade as a result of the extra fees. Each year, they had given themselves large bonuses, money gotten from the unfair fees. Their bonuses were larger than most workers earned in ten years. The settlement didn't require them to give back any of their bonuses or big salaries.

It was astonishing how the laws could be so unfair. After the whole C&L debacle, lawmakers were quickly enacting laws so banks couldn't get away with that anymore, but what was done was done. Those executives had grown wealthy.

The more he read, the more he agreed with Cindy that someone should do something about the unfairness.

* * *

Meanwhile, Cindy had another project she was working on, what she thought of as her Save Spider from a Broken Heart project. She'd been paying close attention to both Spider and Natalie, and it was pretty easy to see where things were headed. Spider looked at Natalie with longing and hope. Natalie looked at Spider with sadness and guilt. If they did get together, it would be because Natalie was being nice. That, obviously, would not work for long.

That afternoon, the airline called to tell her that they'd sent a crew back to the island to get all their suitcases. Hers was now at the San Francisco airport and she could pick it up any time. She asked her older brother Mark for a ride to the airport so she wouldn't have to lug the suitcase on subways and buses. He said sure. She figured all their suitcases were there. Alexis, though, was the only one of the Knights of the Square Table who lived near Cindy in the Sunset district. She called Alexis and offered to get her suitcase for her.

"Thanks!" Alexis said. "My mom was about to go get a Zipcar. I'll tell her she doesn't have to."

Once Cindy and Mark had gotten the suitcases from the airport, she asked him to take hers home, and drop her and Alexis's suitcase off at Alexis's house. She told him she'd take the bus home.

She lugged Alexis's suitcase up the five steps to the door to Alexis's building, then rang the doorbell to her apartment. Moments later, she heard Alexis bounding down the steps. Alexis opened the door and looked around. "Where's your brother?"

"He had stuff to do so I told him I'd take the bus home."

"Come on in," Alexis said. Together they lugged Alexis's suitcase up the flight of stairs to Alexis's apartment. Then Alexis wheeled it inside. "Let's put it in here," she said, and pulled the suitcase into her bedroom. Once inside her room, Alexis opened her suitcase. The clothes inside smelled of the island— that crisp smell of snow and rocks.

"They got everything off the plane belonging to the passengers," Cindy said. "Then they stripped the plane of anything valuable and worth hauling away. The shell of the plane is still there."

"That makes sense, I guess," Alexis said.

Thinking about the plane abandoned there on the island filled Cindy with a strange sadness.

"There's something I want to tell you," Cindy said. "But I don't want Spider to know I said anything."

Now she had Alexis's full attention. "Sit down," Alexis said.

"Thanks." Cindy sat on the desk chair. Alexis sat on her bed.

"So tell me!" Alexis said.

"I'll just come right out and say it," Cindy said. "I think Spider likes you. Actually, I *know* he does."

"Likes *me*? What are you talking about?"

"I mean, *really* likes you. You know what I mean."

"Get out!" Alexis said. "He likes Natalie."

"Everyone likes Natalie. She's sweet and pretty. But he feels different about you. You're the only one who really liked climbing those rocks with him."

"Yeah, that was actually sort of fun."

"He also admires the way you stand up for what you believe in."

"But how do you *know*?" Alexis asked.

"A few things he said. Don't tell him I said anything, okay?

"I wouldn't do that," Alexis said. "But are you *sure*?"

"Completely sure." Cindy stood up. "I'd better get going. I have a *ton* of homework."

"I'll walk you out to the bus," Alexis said.

"Don't worry about it, really." She looked at her public transportation app and said, "If I run I can get the next bus!"

Cindy ran down the stairs, with Alexis following. At the front door to the building, Cindy waved bye and kept running. Alexis went back inside.

Instead of going home, Cindy took the bus in the opposite direction, toward North Beach. She changed buses at California Street, and got off at Washington Square. She didn't know exactly where Spider lived, but she knew it was nearby.

She called him on the phone. "Hey," she said when he answered. "I'm over here in Washington Square. Do you have a minute? I want to talk to you."

"Sure," he said. "I'll be there in five."

She sat on a bench directly in front of the Saints Peter and Paul Church, a soaring Romanesque stone cathedral with twin spires. Coit Tower loomed at the top of Telegraph Hill, to her right. The fog had already rolled in and she felt chilly.

When Spider strolled onto the greens, she waved. He came over and sat on the bench. "What's up?" he asked.

She sighed. "Just something I wanted to tell you. Something I think you should know."

He looked instantly concerned. "What?"

"Nothing *bad*," she said. "I just thought you might want to know that Alexis really likes you."

"*Alexis?*" He looked amazed. "She sure doesn't act like it."

"It started when you two did that rock climbing. But she thinks you're in love with Natalie. You know how people are about stuff like this. They don't show it unless someone encourages them. Alexis is proud."

"She's a tough girl," Spider said.

"She's not as tough as she acts. Also, she really admires your sense of fun. I know she wishes she could be a little more carefree."

Cindy stood up. "There's my bus!" The Muni-30 was just then approaching from the direction of the wharf. "I'd better go!"

"See you later," he said.

"Bye!" She turned and ran. She got to the corner just in time to board. The bus was so packed she had to stand, squeezed in so tightly she could hardly hold a railing. She tried to look out the window, but couldn't see much. Spider had probably left, anyway.

She hoped her plan would work. She knew a trick

like this *could* work. It could also result in disaster, or at the very least get her into big trouble with everyone.

5

Cindy, Natalie, and George attended Lowell Alternative High School, a public school with stringent admission requirements. They often ate lunch together. Liam, Spider, and Alexis attended different private schools.

The next day, Cindy stood in the school cafeteria, looking for George. He entered carrying his bagged lunch and waved to her. She waved back, then motioned for him to join her at a table facing the corner.

They sat down together. George said, "I know what you want to talk about. You want to convince me to hack into the C&L website, right?"

"Ask me if I *like* being completely transparent."

"Nah, I know the answer to *that* question. So I'll ask this. What has gotten into you?"

"I don't know," she said.

He was watching her, his eyebrows raised, waiting for her to say something more, obviously unwilling to accept "I don't know" for an answer.

She unwrapped her sandwich and took a bite.

"Maybe we need to get to the bottom of this,"

George said, "and figure out why you want to do more hacking and take such a big chance."

"I'll tell you what I think. After the things we did on the island, and after stopping that war, well, I *like* how it feels to get something done instead of just thinking about how it would be nice to solve the world's problems. It's hard to go back to the way I was before."

"How were you before?"

"You know how I was before. All I ever wanted to do was read. And play chess."

"Reading and playing chess are good," he said, grinning. "Hacking is bad."

"Depends on why you're hacking, right? Besides, do you ever hear of hackers getting caught? I don't."

"Me neither," he said. "I always just hear about how someone got in somewhere and stole a bunch of credit card numbers."

"I really think we should do it," she said. "Alexis won't help. But you and Liam can do it. Think how good it will feel to set that situation right."

He was quiet for a while. She was usually good at reading people, but this time she had no idea at all what he was thinking. What confused her was that he was watching her closely. In his face, she saw the hint of a smile, and a light in his eyes that she had never seen.

Had she known what he was thinking, she would have been very surprised. He was thinking that he liked her. A lot. He liked how her eyes seemed to take in everything. He admired her ideas, and this new desire of hers to take action.

That was when four of George's friends entered the cafeteria. They saw George and Cindy and waved. George waved back and the guys walked over to their table. George smiled and made small talk with them. Cindy, shy with people she didn't know well, particularly guys, mostly just listened.

* * *

On Friday of the following week, Liam, George, and Cindy were sitting at a picnic table in Alamo Square. The day was sunny and mild. Sometimes you get so used to fog in San Francisco, particularly in late spring and early summer, that sunshine feels like pure magic. The view of the city from the hillside was gorgeous. Instead of going to Lafayette Park, which was closer to Liam's house, they'd come here.

Their picnic table was directly in front of the iconic Painted Ladies, a row of ornately painted San Francisco–style Victorians with a stunning view of the city spread out beyond. Liam had lived in San Francisco all his life, but he still found this view of the city both startling and calming, particularly after so many frustrating hours in front of a computer screen.

"The person who should be here is Spider," Cindy said. "What we did was basically his idea."

Cindy, Liam, and George had spent every afternoon for the past week in the third-floor room of Liam's house, in front of computers. It had taken that long to figure out how to hack into the computer system of the C&L. Well, George and Liam had figured out how to hack into the bank's computers. Cindy didn't know enough about computers to help much. It would have been easier with Alexis. Alexis knew more about coding than they did.

Initially they planned to hack into the bank computer system and distribute the entire balance, all the money the bank had kept in unfair fees, but once they got in, they could find only about $400,000 not in individual, private accounts. Of course, they wanted to move the bank's money, not money belonging to private people—unless they could find accounts belonging to the bank executives. They would have had no qualms redistributing their large bonuses.

They distributed the entire $400,000 to homeless shelters, food banks for the poor, prison reform organizations, and save-the-environment groups. They set aside $15,000 for Veronica's bail. Why should Veronica have to be in jail for petty theft when those bank executives stole millions?

Liam breathed deeply. He felt remarkably at ease and restful. The park was so tranquil, set on a hillside, with tennis courts at the top of the hill, trimmed lawns, and views of the city. The city sparkled in the sunlight, glistening and white.

"I hate to be the one to mention this," Liam said, "but there's always a chance we'll get caught."

"I don't think we will," George said.

"Me, neither," Cindy said. "We got rid of the

computer we used."

They'd used one of the laptop computers Liam's parents got as a demo model. That particular computer was now buried in a dumpster, washed of any fingerprints.

"I guess it's time to tell the others what we did," Cindy said. "Alexis will have a meltdown, even when she understands that we have the $15,000 to pay Veronica's bail. *If* there's some way to do it without the money being traced."

"I'll call a meeting," George said, "as soon as everyone can make it."

"Let's meet here when we tell them," Liam said.

"Yeah," Cindy said. "This park is *so* nice."

* * *

The soonest everyone could make it was Friday after school. On Wednesday Natalie had a dental appointment. On Thursday George had to translate a conference for his parents.

On Friday, they all six sat at the same picnic table in Alamo Park. That day, too, was sunny and mild. Liam brought a box of pastries from a bakery near his house.

Alexis's response was predictable. "You did *what?* Have you gone nuts?"

"Maybe," Cindy said. "I worry about that. But things are so wrong."

"I *get* that the system isn't fair," Alexis said. "But now we're *outlaws*. We're *bank robbers*! This is serious stuff."

"You're not a bank robber," George pointed out. "Me and Liam and Cindy are bank robbers."

"I'm whatever you call the person who helps the robbers, or who knows about it," Alexis said.

"An accomplice," said Cindy, the girl with the million-dollar vocabulary.

"I don't appreciate being an accomplice," Alexis said. "My parents didn't even want me to *visit* a jail without them there. Jeez, guys. How are they going to feel visiting me in prison?"

"We're not going to prison," Liam said. "I promise."

"How do you know?" Alexis demanded.

"I just know," Liam said.

"The problem," said Cindy, "is there is no *legal* way to set the situation right. The only way to really change things to make them fair is to use unconventional methods."

"*Unconventional* methods?" Alexis said. "That's a fancy word for committing crimes."

"Do you know what a crime is?" George asked Alexis.

"*Yes*, I know what a crime is," Alexis said. "Do I have stupid written on my forehead? A crime is something wrong."

"Nope," George said. "A crime is something against the law. Not everything wrong is a crime, and not everything that is a crime is wrong. That's the real problem with all the prisons, Alexis. Mostly the wrong people are inside."

"Give me one example of something that is a

crime that isn't wrong," Alexis said.

"That's easy," said George. "Before the Civil War, it was a crime to help slaves escape. Now people who helped slaves escape are heroes. Do you want a hundred more examples? How about two hundred?"

"All right," Alexis said. "Name something that is really, really wrong, something that hurts a lot of people, but isn't a crime."

"That's easy, too," George said. "What about what those bank executives did? That wasn't a crime. That's how they got away with it. What about the bomb on Hiroshima? If dropping that bomb was a crime, as you yourself said, we live in very criminal country."

Alexis crossed her arms over her chest. "Good luck running for president with *that* attitude," she said.

"I'm not sure anymore about that," George said. "I'm not sure I *want* to be president. Besides, what are the chances? About one in a million. And even the president can't do all that much. Just like all those save-the-world organizations. The president can spend years and years working on a problem without making much progress, and then someone else can come along and just undo everything he did."

"You know," Natalie said, "I don't *feel* like we're outlaws. I feel like George and Liam and Cindy are Robin Hoods. They stole from the thieving rich and gave to the poor."

"And we're their merry men," Spider said. "And

merry girls."

Liam turned and looked at the city. He realized he felt light and happy.

"I like being a Robin Hood," Natalie said. "Or I guess, in my case, one of the merry girls."

"You're not scared?" Alexis asked her.

"No," Natalie said. "I'm not scared. I know I should be, but I'm not."

* * *

Liam walked home with a spring in step. He turned the corner onto his street and stopped abruptly at the sight in front of him. All the lights in his house were on. He'd turned them off before he left. It was five thirty. His parents were rarely home before seven.

His heart was suddenly pounding so hard he felt short of breath. He walked briskly to the door, and used his house key to let himself into the foyer. He hung up his backpack, then walked up the steps to the living room. His parents were at the table. He sat down.

"What's going on?" Liam asked.

"Two FBI officers came to my office," Liam's father said. "They had a warrant to confiscate our computers."

Liam allowed his shock to show, but tried to hide his fear. No reaction at all would make his parents very suspicious.

"What did you do?" Liam said.

"I called our lawyer," said Liam's father. "She referred us to the top criminal defense attorney in the city. The criminal defense lawyer contacted the officers for us, and explained that there was a mistake. No criminal activity occurred here. They reached an agreement. The officers would take our computers, but would not do any searching—they would not even turn them on—until our lawyer had a chance to examine the search warrant and meet with them Monday morning."

Liam frowned, doing his best to look confused.

"I'm sure it's all a mistake," said Liam's mother. "Our lawyer will get to the bottom of this." There was the slightest quiver in her voice.

The doorbell rang. Liam gave a start.

"That's probably the take-out order," Liam's father said, standing up. "I'll get it."

Liam's dad went down the stairs. His mother went into the kitchen and took dishes from the cabinets and utensils from the drawers.

"I'll go wash up," Liam said. He ran lightly upstairs to the small bathroom connected to his bedroom and took his cell phone out of his pocket. He knew better than to send a text or email containing incriminating information, so he ran the water in the sink to drown out the sound, just in case one of his parents came upstairs. He called George.

George answered on the third ring.

"The FBI was here," Liam said in a coarse whisper.

George gasped. "What did they do?"

"They took all our computers. They're not going to search them until Monday after our lawyer talks to them."

"But they can't get actual proof of what we did without the computer we used, right?"

"I don't *think* so," Liam said. "They clearly know something happened from this house. If they don't have actual proof that it was us, we can probably say someone hacked in here and used our Internet access. The problem is if someone starts asking me questions, it's all over. I'm a terrible liar."

"Your parents didn't ask you *anything*?"

He opened his door to make sure his parents were still downstairs. He heard them in the dining room talking as they set the table.

He closed the bathroom door again and whispered, "It would never occur to them in a million years that I did something against the law."

"Maybe we could figure out how to put the money back." George was talking so softly Liam could scarcely hear him.

"We'd have to figure it out by Monday," Liam said. "And all our computers are gone."

"We *could* just confess. We'll probably get sent to prison, but we're just kids, and it isn't like we kept any for ourselves. I'll bet we get off easy. We're also famous, don't forget."

"That could make things worse," Liam said. "And confessing is out of the question. I'm not going to prison, bro. Besides, I promised Alexis nobody's going to jail."

"Yeah," George said. "I'm with you. I'll call the others and tell them. I'll call you back later."

6

George hung up and sat perfectly still. He was at his desk, alone in his room, with the door closed. He went to his bedroom door, opened it, and looked out. As usual his home was full of people. Two of his uncles were watching television. They liked watching television here because the screen was bigger than in their apartments. From the kitchen came the sound of pans clanging. Several of his cousins were playing a very noisy game that involved running up and down the stairs leading from the kitchen to the garage. A few other cousins and his younger siblings were in the yard downstairs, playing with a beach ball—the only ball they were allowed to play with because it couldn't break any windows.

Clearly nobody had heard his side of the conversation he'd just had with Liam. But he couldn't keep taking the chance. The walls were thin. Anyone could walk into his room any time, or listen at the door. There was just no place in this apartment he could talk in private. The streets, always crowded at this time of day, wouldn't be any better.

He slipped his phone into his jeans pocket and

walked into the living room. He crossed in front of his uncles to get to the front door. "Be back in a minute," he said, as casually as he could manage.

One of his uncles waved. The other wasn't paying attention.

Once outside, he ran down the three flights to the street. He cut across Kearny Street and headed toward the Willy Wong playground. At the park, a group of children were on the equipment. A few parents pushed children on the swings. Another group of children and an elderly couple sat at a nearby picnic table. Three older men sat on one of the benches. Otherwise, the park was empty, but very noisy, nestled between two busy streets. Overhead was a large billboard reminding drivers that honking doesn't make the traffic move faster.

A bench was off by itself, under the spreading branches of a purple leaf plum tree. George walked over to the bench, pulled his phone out of his pocket, and sat down.

He needed to make a phone call, but he wasn't ready. First he had to think the situation over.

He knew where they needed to go. There was one place on earth they could call their very own, a place they could hide and live the way they wanted to.

Being on that island was like going all the way back in time, before the whole world got so screwed up.

He could think of only one way to get to an island in the middle of the ocean two hundred miles off the coast of Iceland. It certainly wasn't what Don had in mind when he'd said to call him if he ever needed anything. Most likely he'd refuse, so they needed a backup plan. The only alternative he could think of was to head north, over the Canadian border, and find a place they could hide and survive.

As the reality of the situation dawned on George, he fully understood what running away meant. He would be an exile. A fugitive forever. His whole life. This wasn't like going on a camping trip or vacation. Once they left, they could never come back.

He figured he'd call Cindy first. May as well make the easiest call first. She answered on the first ring. "George? What's going on?" She didn't even say hello.

He told her about the FBI at Liam's house and what he thought they should do.

"Let me think for a minute," Cindy said.

From the other side of the park came the squeals of children playing on the swings. From the streets came the sounds of cars and buses. The noises were normal and ordinary, as if his life were not being completely turned upside down at this very moment.

"All right," Cindy said. "I think we all need to meet early tomorrow morning. Everyone needs to come prepared to run away, and leave some kind of note to keep our families from calling the police. Leave false clues pointing in another direction if you can think of any."

George was about to tell her that he didn't think the police looked too hard for teenage runaways. Then he remembered they weren't ordinary teenage runaways. After Monday they may very well be wanted by the FBI.

"You know," she said, "I have relatives who would say that we are flat-out wrong. They'd say the problem is this country does *too much* to coddle the poor and petty criminals like Veronica. They're all for war, as long as they think America is fighting on the right side. They don't think cleaning up the environment is their problem."

"That's why I can't stand the thought anymore of going into politics," George said. "I just don't want to argue about it for the rest of my life. It seems too tiring, and hopeless. For all I know, your relatives may be right. And that's just too depressing."

"I don't *think* they're right," Cindy said. "At least, I don't want them to be right." After a pause, she asked, "So what do we do now?"

"I think first we have to get to Canada," he said. "We can't ask Don to take us over the border. That could really get him into trouble. And he may not take us back to the island. I'd totally understand if he says no way. But at least we'll be in Canada."

"Yeah," Cindy said. "We can find a place on the coast to hide and figure out how to survive."

"How are we going to get across the border?" he asked.

"We have our letters allowing us international travel with the chess team. The letters restrict us to traveling in Europe and North America, so we're okay there. We need to do some research on crossing into Canada."

"Be careful with any searches," he said. "Don't

search on any device you're leaving in the house. You can't really clear the search. Someone can figure out what websites you were looking at. And we can't use our phones after we leave San Francisco. Anyone can trace our location if our phones are on. But bring your phone so nobody can read all your stuff."

"Okay," she said.

"I better get back home," George said. "I don't think I have time to call the others."

"I'll take over. I'll tell everyone to meet at Powell Street Station tomorrow morning, at the main entrance by the cable cars. At 8:00 a.m."

"Sounds good," George said. "Talk to you soon."

* * *

Natalie was in the living room, looking in a drawer for a spiral notebook, when Cindy called. There was so much noise that she didn't hear the phone ringing. Her house was always noisy, particularly when the windows were open, as they were now. From the street came the sound of cars honking, people shouting, and buses clanging. Eleven people lived in Natalie's house: her parents, her six siblings, and her maternal grandparents. The house had two bedrooms upstairs, in the main part of the house, plus the basement and garage had been converted into four bedrooms.

"Natalie!" one of her brothers shouted. "Your phone's ringing!"

"I'll get it!" she shouted back. She ran into the room she shared with three of her sisters. She found her phone in her backpack.

By then she had missed Cindy's call. None of her sisters were home, so she could close her bedroom door and be alone. She called Cindy back. "What's up?" she asked, when Cindy answered.

"A bit of a problem," Cindy said. Natalie listened as Cindy told her about the FBI at Liam's house, and what she and George thought they should do.

"I think this was meant to happen," Natalie said. "If there's such a thing as fate, we're *supposed* to go back."

You'd think Natalie would have felt afraid, but she didn't. It had never in her life occurred to her to run away, and here she was ready to go without a backwards glance.

"Do you think we can survive on a cold island?" Cindy asked. "Or hiding in Canada?"

"I think I can do that easier than I can get used to federal prison."

"The real question is whether we can get all the way to Canada without getting caught."

"We've done harder things," Natalie said. "I guess I should start thinking about what to bring."

"Bring any money you have. Don't forget your passport and international travel letter. And think up a good excuse for being gone. Leave a note that will keep your family from calling the police. Bring any info you think we'll need." She told Natalie what George had said about their phones, and not being able to completely clear searches.

Natalie sighed deeply. "When my mother bought

me the phone, she made me promise that wherever I was, I'd answer if she calls."

"You won't be able to do that."

"Yeah," Natalie said. "I know."

"So you're okay with leaving?" Cindy asked. "The ones who could really get into trouble are me, George, and Liam. We're the only ones who really need to go."

"Not really. If you, George, and Liam leave, and the FBI has all Liam's computers, they'll know a lot about what we've been up to. Besides, if you leave, they'll come find me, Alexis, and Spider and ask us lots of questions. It will be sort of awkward."

"That's true," Cindy said. "I guess I got everyone into trouble. I'm really sorry."

"I understand what you did, and why. I'm okay with leaving. Besides, I like what Liam said about how living on the island is like going all the way back in time, before things got so messed up."

"I liked that, too," Cindy said. "Who expected Liam to be so poetic?"

"I was so happy after we averted that war," Natalie said. "Then, when fighting broke out again over there, it started to seem like the whole thing was just hopeless. Then, when we realized the extent of all those problems, and that there was really nothing we could do, well, it really felt discouraging, didn't it?"

"I thought so. And now we're in trouble. And I need to call Alexis. I'm not looking forward to it."

"She's not going to like it," Natalie said. "Call me

back and tell me what she says. I can talk to her if you want me to."

* * *

Cindy decided to tell Alexis in person. All she had to do to get to Alexis's house was take the N-Judah streetcar up the hill. She could be there in twenty minutes.

Cindy asked her mom if she could go visit Alexis for a little while. Her mom said fine, be back before dark. Then she called Alexis to see if it was okay if she stopped by. Alexis also said fine, no problem.

Cindy arrived at the apartment building and buzzed Alexis's doorbell. Alexis came bounding down the stairs. She opened the door and asked, "What's the matter?"

"Come on out," Cindy said. "Let's walk somewhere."

As soon as they started off down the sidewalk, Alexis said, "You guys got caught, huh?"

Cindy felt impressed that Alexis had guessed. "It looks that way." She turned to see how Alexis was taking it. Alexis was scowling.

"How'd you get caught?" Alexis asked.

Cindy told her the whole story. When she finished, Alexis said, "I guess we're going north."

It was hard for Cindy to read Alexis's tone of voice. She didn't sound as angry as Cindy expected.

"I looked up what we did," Cindy said. "You were right. We're guilty of more than one federal crime. We should have listened to you."

"If you'd listened to me the first time, there might have been a nuclear war. If you'd listened to me the second time, nobody would be in trouble right now, but the bank would have even more money it didn't deserve and the homeless shelters would have less."

Cindy considered this. "Are you mad at us?"

"Yes, I'm mad at you. I'm mad that you went around me. That really wasn't right. Instead of going around me, or just telling me *you're outvoted*, the way George did when we hacked into the Democratic Republic website, you could have discussed it until I felt comfortable. That might have been nice."

"You're right, we should have," Cindy said. "I'm sorry."

"I want a change in the rules," Alexis said. "From now on, no more majority vote. All important decisions have to be unanimous. No going around me."

"That's fair," Cindy said.

"We need to make sure everyone agrees to the new rule," Alexis said.

"I think we can do that in a text," Cindy said. She sent a group text: "*Alexis wants to change the rules. No more majority rules. All decisions have to be unanimous from now on. Okay?*"

All four quickly responded and agreed.

They resumed walking. "So anyway," Cindy said, "we put the bail money for Veronica in an account where we can get it."

"I guess I have to be the one to go to Sacramento and try to bail her out. I'm the one who knows her aunt Tammy."

"Once you have anything to do with that $15,000, you'll probably be more than just an accomplice."

"Yeah, I get that," Alexis said. "What's the difference at this point?"

"Can we bail someone out on a Saturday?" Cindy asked.

"I don't know," Alexis asked. "Let's ask Professor Google." She took out her phone, opened her browser to Google, and typed, "Can you bail someone out of jail on a Saturday in California?" She glanced at the first several entries that came up and said, "Friday night and Saturday are the most common times to bail someone out of jail." She looked at Cindy and said, "I guess that makes sense, right? People are out getting into trouble on weekends."

At the end of the block was a low stone wall separating the street from a park. Once there, they sat on the wall.

"I did some reading," Cindy said. "For federal crimes like ours, there are things called *mandatory minimum sentences*. The judge can't let us off easy even if he wants to. Plus they'd probably put us on trial as adults. If we stick around, we'll be in prison for a very long time."

"That's why we're not sticking around," Alexis said.

* * *

Packing was hard for Spider because his parents

spent all evening in the living room. He really wanted to get the first aid kit from the hallway closet, but he couldn't without them seeing him. His backpack, hidden now in his closet, was completely stuffed. Inside was a winter camping sleeping bag, the thermal underwear he wore while accompanying his grandfather on the fishing boat, and his ski coat. He had an extra satchel with clothing hidden downstairs by the back door. After packing the satchel, he had just enough room for the fishing gear from the garage: heavy-duty fishing nets, lines, and hooks. He also brought his mesh laundry bag.

He really wanted that first aid kit even though he wasn't sure how he'd fit it in. His mother was the type to worry, so the kit was complete, containing everything from antibiotic cream to an emergency medical manual.

He was in his room, sitting on his bed, listening to the sounds in the house, waiting for his chance. He heard his older brother tell his parents good night. Then came footsteps on the stairs as his brother went down to his bedroom. His older brother slept in the converted bedroom behind the garage. His younger brother, who shared Spider's room and slept in the top bunk, was already asleep.

At last, Spider's father also went downstairs, probably to make sure the doors were closed and locked. When his mother went into the bathroom, he seized the opportunity, slipped from his bedroom, and snatched the first aid kit from the closet. He slid back into his room and stuffed the first aid kit into his backpack, then shoved the backpack back into his closet, and shut the closet door.

He heard his dad come up the stairs. He poked his head out of his room and said, "Good night, Mom! Good night, Dad!"

They both said good night. He closed his door, turned out his light, and got into bed. He continued listening to the sounds in the house, expecting his parents to go into the kitchen, as they usually did. His mother liked a cup of tea before bed. Soon he heard sounds from the kitchen.

Then he was startled to hear footsteps outside his door, followed by a soft knock. "Come in," he said.

The door opened and his father stood in the doorway, silhouetted by the light from the living room. He entered the room and sat on his bed.

His father *never* came into his room like this anymore. He used to, of course, when Spider was younger, but he hadn't for a long time. Spider felt alarmed.

His father patted his shoulder and whispered, "What are you up to, son?"

Spider swallowed. His mouth felt suddenly dry. "What do you mean?"

"Are you planning to go somewhere you're not telling us about?"

"No," Spider whispered. "What makes you think that?" He was glad they were whispering instead of speaking aloud. His throat felt very tight. "I'm going to hang out with Liam at his house tomorrow."

"Your mother thinks you're up to something.

Look, there's not much I can do to keep you from sneaking out if you take wild ideas into your head. You're fifteen. I can't very well chain you up."

Spider felt it would be hard to speak past the lump in his throat. He wondered what would happen if he told his father everything, the whole truth. He was pretty sure his father would understand, and sympathize.

But Liam and the others didn't *want* to confess. They didn't want to risk prison. They wanted to run away, and Spider needed to be with his buddies. Liam, Alexis, and George might be able to figure out how to hack into computers, and Cindy was full of ideas, but he was the one who could best survive on a cold, rocky island. He was easily the strongest. More to the point, if they were going to an island in the North Atlantic, or even if they got no farther than Canada's west coast, he *wanted* to be with them. He couldn't think of anywhere he'd rather be—as much as he hated having to leave home.

"All I can say," his father said, "is please don't do anything foolish."

"I wouldn't, Dad."

"You can always call me if you need something. If you're in trouble and need help, I won't ask any questions. I'll come get you wherever you are."

The lump in Spider's throat grew larger. Guilt didn't even begin to describe what he felt. "Thanks, Dad."

His father gave him a tight hug, then patted him again on the shoulder. "You're a good kid. You've always been a good kid. I trust you not to do anything risky." He stood up, walked from the room, and quietly closed the door behind him.

Spider lay still, staring into the darkness, waiting for the ache in his chest to subside. He wanted to talk to someone. What startled him was that the person he wanted to talk to was Alexis. Natalie was the type to say something soothing. Alexis was the person you could count on for the cold, hard truth. Earlier, when he'd talked to Cindy, she told him how Alexis responded. Alexis never said anything like *I told you so*, and, in fact, was eager to leave.

This surprised him. He took out his phone and called her.

"Spider!" she whispered. "Hold on a minute."

He assumed she was going somewhere she could talk.

When she came back to the phone, she said, "What a shock, right?"

"For us it's a shock," he said. "You predicted this."

"I guess I always expect the worst," she said. "It's a bad habit."

"My dad just came into my room. He knows I'm up to something."

"What did he say?"

"He said I can call him if I get into trouble or need anything. He said he won't ask any questions."

"My parents are pretty sympathetic," Alexis said, "but I doubt even they'll appreciate the fine distinction between being an ordinary bank robber and a modern-day Robin Hood. Speaking of that, I'll be a Robin Hood tomorrow, sort of. I'm going to try to bail Veronica out with that bank money."

"If you get caught," he said, "remember you're Robin Hood and not the Lone Ranger. We're all in this together."

"I better go. If I stay in the garage too long my family will wonder what I'm doing."

"See you tomorrow," he said. "Good luck."

"Bye," she said, and disconnected.

His plan had been to leave the house at 7:40, telling his parents that Liam was already awake so he was heading over to his house for the day. But under the circumstances, that wouldn't work. He couldn't leave the house with a full backpack and an extra satchel, not after that conversation with his father.

He set the alarm on his phone to vibrate at 4:00, and slipped the phone under his pillow. He'd just have to leave the house early, and spend a few hours walking the streets until 8:00. He saw no alternative.

* * *

Liam told his parents he was going to bed early. He said good night and switched off his light. Once he was in darkness, though, he turned on his electronic tablet. Using the Internet connection on his tablet, he read everything he could find about surviving in a cold climate.

The good thing about going all the way back in time before things got so screwed up was you could create your own little community that wasn't screwed up. The bad part was you had nothing else but what you could carry with you.

Once he thought about it, he decided it *was* a little strange that his parents hadn't asked him any questions. It occurred to him that his parents didn't really know him. All they saw when they looked at him was their brilliant straight-A son, talented in music and chess, the well-behaved boy teachers had been praising since preschool. They had no idea how lonely he'd been all of his life, or that in joining the chess team, he found companionship for the first time.

He'd turned off his tablet and was staring into the darkness when his phone on the table next to him vibrated. This evening, he'd already talked to George twice, Spider once, and Alexis once. He reached for the phone. This time the caller was Cindy.

He clicked the talk button, and whispered, "Cindy?"

"Did I wake you up?" she whispered.

"No," he said.

She sighed. "I just called to say I'm sorry. It's all my fault. If not for me and my ideas, we wouldn't be in this mess."

"If you recall, me and George *liked* the idea. We *wanted* to do it."

"Yeah," she said. "But I'm still feeling bad about the whole thing."

He didn't like hearing the pain in her voice. He searched for a way to make her feel better. "I'm glad I did it," he said. "I'm glad we redistributed that money. I'm glad we got those countries to negotiate."

She sighed. "Even though it may not have done much good."

"That's not your fault," he told her. "Go back to thinking about how we can solve all the world's major problems."

"There's no chance of that," she said.

"Exactly. That's why we're leaving." He paused. "That, and because the FBI will be after us soon."

7

The first train left the Bay Area for Sacramento just before 6:00 a.m. Alexis was on the train with a backpack filled with spare clothing and toiletries. In her handbag were her passport, her international travel letter, and her wallet, containing $450. When she'd started babysitting, her parents helped her open an account so she could deposit her earnings and her birthday money. Alexis withdrew the full amount that morning. George warned everyone that if they were going to withdraw money, do it in San Francisco because their parents would be able to see the location of the withdrawal.

The jail opened at 7:00. She'd called Tammy the evening before. They planned to meet at the train station.

Alexis watched out the window as the train pulled across the Carquinez Bridge, heading northeast out of the Bay Area. At least Sacramento was the right general direction. A look at Google Maps had shown her that the easiest way to the Canadian border was north on Interstate 5, one of the freeways that passed through Sacramento.

What an irony that she was the one who hadn't wanted to break the law, and here she was, going to Sacramento to bail Veronica out of jail with stolen money.

If you get caught, remember you're Robin Hood and not the Lone Ranger, Spider had said.

She didn't intend to get caught. Okay, she didn't have the slightest idea what she was doing, but her plan was to figure it out and be careful.

At 7:35, the train pulled into the station in Sacramento. She gathered her stuff and walked through the station. Once outside on the street, she squinted from the bright sunlight.

Tammy pulled up in her van. Alexis opened the door, slid into the front seat, and put her stuff on the floor.

They greeted each other. Then Tammy pulled out of the train station parking lot, onto a street that was almost deserted. "So how on earth did you get the money?"

"My family is rich," Alexis said. "I got it from my grandmother. She gives me anything I want." As Alexis said the words, she realized they sounded completely preposterous.

Tammy turned around and shot her a look. "Oh, come on."

"It's true." *Darn,* she thought. First mistake, coming without George. He was much better at fooling adults.

"Wanna know what I think?" Tammy said. "I think you pulled some hanky-panky to get that money. What's all that stuff you're carrying?"

Alexis considered how to answer. If Tammy was already onto her, what chance did she have of pulling anything off with law enforcement officers, who were trained to detect lying kids? Being a successful outlaw appeared to be much harder than, say, maintaining a perfect grade point average.

Tammy drove a few blocks, then stopped in front of a grassy park with a beautifully manicured rose garden. Over the trees Alexis could see the domed capitol building.

"I thought so," Tammy said. "What do I say when the police show up?"

"If you never touch the money," Alexis said, "how can you get into trouble?"

"You don't really think a kid can bail someone out of jail with $15,000 without raising questions, do you?"

Alexis considered this. "So what do we do?"

"Give me the money, or access to the money, and I'll go and do it. Meanwhile, you stay here. Right now I don't know anything, so there isn't much I can say. They'd never believe some kid handed it to me and said it came from her rich grandmother, but that's exactly what happened so far. If I'm not back in one hour, you leave. I assume you have money for a cab back to the train station. I mean, having a wealthy grandmother and all."

"Just don't give them my name for twenty-four hours, okay?" It seemed to Alexis that was plenty of time to get over the border.

"That's easy enough," Tammy said. "I won't talk without my lawyer, and my lawyer isn't available until Monday. So where are you going? Canada?"

"What are you? A mind reader?"

Tammy laughed. "Some things are obvious. Like a kid running away. Besides, I know how you've been feeling lately. My generation did a lot of this sort of thing, rejecting society's values, thinking we could run away and figure out how to live better lives."

"Could you?" Alexis asked.

"Of course! How hard is *that*?"

Alexis smiled. She didn't expect to be smiling this morning.

"All right," Tammy said. "If I'm going to do this deed, I want to do it early, while I'm up for it."

"Thanks," Alexis said.

"Don't thank me. You're the one doing this for my niece. Speaking of which, did I mention? You're taking Veronica with you. To Canada. Got that?"

"Right," Alexis said. Suddenly it made sense, particularly because—unbeknownst to Tammy—their final destination was not Canada. At least she hoped not. She wanted to be in the Gulf Stream, not Canada's west coast. Where they were going, Veronica could steal all she wanted without danger of spending years and years in a prison. Besides, there'd be nothing to steal.

"If Veronica wants to go," Alexis said.

"She'll want to go, trust me. The alternative is years in prison."

8

Liam arrived at Powell Street Station the next morning with a backpack and a guitar. It was 8:07. Spider, George, Natalie, and Cindy were already there, waiting for him in the courtyard just outside the station at the foot of the stairs leading to the cable car entrance. At this hour, the Powell Street subway station always reeked of urine and sweat because of all the homeless people who slept just inside the entrance. From the street came the clanging of the cable cars. He supposed by now there was already a long line of tourists waiting to get on.

"Good thinking," Spider said to him, "a guitar."

Liam looked to see if Spider was being sarcastic. He wasn't. Liam grinned and said, "It's the perfect accompaniment for *kum-ba-ya*."

"Alexis just called on Veronica's supercool aunt Tammy's phone," Cindy told Liam. "They got Veronica out. Tammy had some scary moments, but she did it. It looks like we're taking Veronica with us, and Tammy is driving us to Canada. No need to buy bus tickets. We're going in style, in a flower-power hippie van."

"Cool!" Spider said. "Liam can play his guitar and we can all sing *freedom's just another word for nothing left to lose*."

"It's perfect because we won't have to answer questions on the bus about where we're going and why we're traveling alone," Cindy said. "Not that George wouldn't be able to handle the questions just fine."

George cleared his throat. "Ladies and gentlemen, boys and girls. Members of the San Francisco all-star chess team. We are about to embark on a great adventure. First stop, Sacramento."

They entered the subway station, and went through the turnstiles to the escalator leading to the rapid transit trains. George noticed Cindy was completely weighed down. In addition to her very full backpack, she was carrying two nylon bags reaching almost to her knees, one slung over each shoulder.

"I'll help you," George told Cindy. He took one of the bags. Spider took the other.

"What do you have in here?" Spider asked. "Bricks?"

"Books," she said.

"I thought you said to travel light!" Spider said. He looked inside each of the bags. Sure enough, both bags were stuffed with paperbacks. The ones he could see were classics, the kind you read in honors classes and college: Plato's *Republic*, Seneca's *Letters from a Stoic*, Nietzsche's *Beyond Good and Evil*. He also spotted a few novels: *Middlemarch* and *Mrs. Dalloway*.

The largest book was *The Complete Works of William Shakespeare.*

"Heavy stuff!" Spider said.

"Depends on how you look at it," Cindy said. "If you consider how lightweight each paperback is and how many words are packed into each one, you can see that I'm bringing the most words possible per pound."

Spider looked at her, amused. "You're planning to read all of those?"

"Why not?" Cindy asked. "Maybe if we read all these books we might be able to figure out what's wrong with the world."

"I guess books are more important to our survival than, say, extra warm clothes and a portable stove," Spider said. "You're a very practical girl, Cindy."

"Go ahead and joke," Cindy said. "But on those cold winter days by the fire, when you're tired of singing *freedom's just another word for nothing left to lose,* you'll be glad I brought books."

"But these are the books nobody wants to read!" Spider said.

"Speak for yourself," Cindy said. "Just because you're cool doesn't mean other people don't want to embrace their nerdiness. I brought all the books I could find in the heavy department." She glanced at Spider and said, "Heavy in the symbolic sense."

"I'm a nerd!" Spider said. "I never said I wasn't!"

"How did you get out of the house with these?" George asked. "Didn't someone wonder?"

"I hid the bags outside by the garbage cans."

The subway train came, and they boarded it. The train was only about half full, so they got seats together.

"Everyone needs to power down their phones," Liam whispered. "From now on, no Internet unless we find a library or Internet cafe or something. Pop out your batteries just to be safe."

"How are we going to call Don?" Natalie asked.

"I have that prepaid phone," George said. "I still have seventeen minutes."

They settled in their seats and powered down their phones. George reached into one of Cindy's book bags. He pulled out *Nicomachean Ethics* and started reading. He didn't get very far before he closed the book, turned to Cindy, and said, "Who *was* this Aristotle guy? He's *wrong*."

"Aristotle happened to be one of the greatest philosophers who ever lived," Cindy told him.

"Seriously?" George asked. "Right here at the beginning he writes, 'Every human activity aims at some end that we consider good.' I don't get how dumping poisons in the oceans aims at some good. Or sabotaging peace."

"Notice," Cindy said, "he writes, 'Every human activity aims at some end we *consider* good.' He doesn't say it *is* good."

Natalie, sitting just behind them, leaned forward and said, "It's very wise when you think about it. Everything people do, they *think* is good. Most of the time they're wrong, but they don't know that."

"Like some of the things we've done lately," Cindy said.

"Sorry," Liam said, "but I don't think it's true that everything people do, they think is good. When a jerk is being a jerk, he knows it. Do you really think those crazy dudes who walk into crowded places and start shooting think they're doing good?"

"In their own minds they probably do," Natalie said.

"My buddies," Spider said proudly to nobody in particular, "discussing Aristotle early on a Saturday morning."

George put *Nicomachean Ethics* back into the bag, then pulled out *The Prince* by Nicolo Machiavelli. He spent the ride to Richmond engrossed in the book. At one point he looked up and said, "Man, this is some outrageous stuff!"

In Richmond, they transferred to Amtrak. They found five seats together, two seats on either side of the aisle, and one behind. The train was even less crowded than the rapid transit trains, but there were still too many people around to talk about the things that really needed to be talked about, like what they intended to tell the officers at the Canadian border. And what they were going to do if Don said: *Are you out of your friggin' minds? I am not helping runaway fugitives—even if I do owe you a big favor.*

Liam pulled out a travel chess set. Soon he and Spider were absorbed in a game. Cindy watched them play. Natalie looked into one of the bags and selected *Middlemarch* and started reading.

When the train rolled into the station in Sacramento, they gathered their backpacks, satchels, and bags and walked through the station to the street. The sun was bright, the glare on the street blinding.

"Man, it's *hot* here!" Spider said. "It feels like we're in an oven!"

"Yeah," Natalie said. "Where's that cool misty ocean breeze?"

"Don't worry," Spider told her. "Where we're going, there will be plenty of cool misty breezes."

"Look!" Cindy said. "There's the van!"

A lavender-colored van pulled up in front of them. Veronica was in the passenger seat, and a gray-haired woman was driving.

"Hi, I'm Tammy," the driver said through the open window. She had a friendly expression, and an easy, cheerful smile. She was so unlike the gloomy and dour Veronica it was hard to believe they were related.

Alexis slid open the backdoor and said, "Everyone in!"

They piled in with all their stuff. The van seated seven people, which meant they'd have to be a little squished. Liam and Spider sat in the middle seats. The three girls and George—who was the smallest of the guys—squeezed into the very backseat meant for three people.

The interior of the van smelled of apples and soap—like someone's kitchen. When George turned to put his backpack into the space behind the third seat, he saw paper grocery bags filled with clothing.

He didn't want to drop his backpack on top of the bags, but he saw no choice. The girls did the same with their backpacks.

"There's a lot of stuff in here," Tammy said. "There's always a lot of stuff in here, but now there's more than usual. We went back to my trailer and loaded up with anything we thought we could use for the drive north, including the food in my part of the fridge."

"This is very nice of you," George said.

"Nothing nice about it," Tammy said. "Don't forget, you're taking Veronica with you. When I was living in this van, I could keep her with me. But I'm sharing a trailer now with three other people. That makes it hard. And now she's looking at fifteen years in prison."

Veronica turned around. She looked George directly in the eye. Her gaze was unwavering. "What are you kids running away from?"

"We're not saying," George said.

"You must be in trouble," Veronica said. "Big trouble, if we're going to Canada."

George smiled at her and very smoothly said, "From what you've seen, do we seem like the kind of kids to get into such big trouble we have to hide in Canada?"

Veronica considered this. A hint of a smile came to her. Natalie, watching, didn't think she'd *ever* seen Veronica smile. "From what I've seen," Veronica said, "nothing you kids could do would surprise me."

"If you have a smart phone," Liam told her, "you

better power it down. If anyone looks for you, they can see your location."

Veronica pulled her phone out of her purse and tossed it into the backseat. Spider caught it.

"Me, too?" Tammy asked.

"Yeah," George said. "It would be a good idea."

Tammy tossed her phone back, too. Spider powered them both down, then removed the batteries.

Tammy veered right onto the freeway under a sign that said, "Interstate 5 North." To the side of the road were clusters of fast-food restaurants and gas stations. The van didn't have air conditioning, so all the windows were down. The wind coming in the windows was hot and dry, like a blast of air from a hair dryer.

"I assume you have a specific destination in Canada," Tammy said, "and a way of living once you're there. But I'm not asking any questions. I'll just assume one of Alexis's rich relatives lives there. All I can say is good for you. Canada is a great place. But they have laws against theft, there, too, so you'll have to keep Veronica out of trouble."

Veronica slouched into her seat and looked at the window.

"We can give you gas money," Liam told Tammy. "We'd been planning to buy a bus ticket for each of us."

"So how did you kids get this kind of money?" Tammy asked. "Rob a bank or something?"

It was obvious from her tone that she considered

bank robbery a preposterous possibility.

"We each brought whatever money we had," George said. "Some of us had hundreds of dollars in savings. Birthday money, Christmas money, stuff like that."

"Yeah, right," Tammy said. "Wanna try telling me that birthday money and Christmas money could cover $15,000 in bail? Never mind. Don't say a word. I don't want to hear a single word. I entirely believe it all came from Alexis's rich grandmother."

"We don't actually have that much left," George said, "after we bailed Veronica out."

Veronica turned around again. This time she looked directly at Alexis. "So how come? How come you're doing this for me?"

"We just wanted to," Alexis said.

"Why?" Veronica asked.

Because we set out to correct all the injustices in the world, and this was as far as we got, Alexis thought. What she said was, "It's very complicated."

"Look," Tammy said. "I know what you kids did for Veronica when that plane was stranded. If not for Alexis and the rest of you, who knows what those people would have done. Ugly things can happen in a situation like that. I'm glad you can take Veronica. We're obviously at the point where I can't do any more for her. My sister came up with the money for that treatment in Switzerland. It was *supposed* to help."

"If you have money in the bank, Veronica," Cindy said, "you better take it out now, before we get too far."

Veronica reached into her wallet and removed a bank card with the blue and gold C&L logo and handed it over her shoulder to Liam.

"There's about $200 in the checking account," Veronica said, "and four weeks' pay in the savings account, about $1,500."

"If we're going to withdraw your cash we'd better do it now," Cindy said, "while we're in Sacramento. When they come looking for you they'll know the location of the withdrawal."

"All right," Tammy said. "There's a bank at the next exit." She changed to the right lane. Just off the freeway, in a cluster of shops, was a C&L branch. Tammy pulled into a parking place and turned off the engine.

Liam handed the card back to Veronica. Tammy and Veronica got out of the car and walked across the parking lot to the bank entrance.

After they were inside, Spider said, "I feel weird, like they're going in to commit robbery or something."

"Yeah," Alexis said. "I know what you mean."

Spider turned around and put his elbow on the back of the seat so he could see everyone at once. "What note did you guys leave?"

Natalie said, "I wrote something like, 'Please don't worry about me. I am fine. Please don't call the police. If you do, I could get into big trouble. I promise I am safe."

"I wrote something like that, too," Liam said. "Thing is, my parents are going to know right away as soon as they find my note that I'm leaving because I'm guilty and the FBI is after me."

"What are they going to do?" George asked.

Liam considered this. "I actually have no clue."

The door to the bank opened. Veronica and Tammy walked out briskly and headed toward the car. When they slid back into their seats, Veronica turned around and handed George a large envelope. He looked inside. It was full of cash.

"Thanks for getting me out of jail," Veronica said. "I always did like you kids. Right from the beginning."

Tammy started up the engine and wheeled the car out of the parking lot, back toward Interstate 5. She turned on the radio. The Who was playing. Tammy turned around and shouted over the radio, "Does anyone mind oldies?"

"I *love* oldies!" Liam said.

"Great!" Tammy said, and turned the volume up even louder. Over the music, she shouted, "A good strong beat helps me focus on driving. Gives me energy."

It wasn't long before they were out of Sacramento, with mostly farmland all around. The terrain was flat in all directions so you could see for miles and miles. On the western horizon was the coastal range. On the eastern horizon were the Sierras, gray and fuzzy in the distance. The Who, on the radio, was singing about their generation, and telling the older folks to fade away.

With the radio on and the windows down, there

was so much noise in the van that the Knights of the Square Table could put their heads together and talk without Veronica and Tammy knowing what they were saying. In fact, talking from the third seat to the front would have required yelling.

From where Cindy sat—between Alexis and the window—she could watch everyone. Mostly she kept her eye on Spider and Alexis. She noticed that they looked at each other often. She felt pleased. Looking, she suspected, was the first step.

"I did some research," Cindy said. "I found addresses for Internet cafes near the border on both sides. I also looked at maps and lists of stores in some of the towns we'll be passing through. I started a list of what we'll need to buy. I already looked up places to shop."

She passed around the list, and the others added to it—or took off an item if it was something they'd brought. Among the items on their final list were sturdy tarps, more matches than they thought they'd ever need in water-tight containers, an ice knife and axe, shovels, and seeds for planting. The bulk of their money would go for sleeping bags that could keep them warm in temperatures way below zero and the right jackets and rain gear.

Several of them, while doing some last-minute research, had learned that it was possible to make cement out of crushed and burned seashells instead of limestone. They didn't know if there would be limestone where they were going, but there would definitely be seashells, so they'd be able to mix mortar for building stone walls. On the list, therefore, was a pan and trowel so they could mix and spread the mortar.

Natalie had found a picture of a sod house, which struck her as perfect for the region. In fact, the caption was "Nordic House." The house was built into the side of the hill, using the sod for a roof, with a stone wall in front and a door. She passed around the picture and they all agreed they'd build such houses when they reached their destination.

"What do we tell them in the store when we're buying thermals?" Natalie said. "Won't it seem weird to shop for this stuff in May?"

"Nah," Alexis said. "If anyone asks, we tell them we're planning ahead and looking for bargains. May is probably when secondhand stores have this stuff."

Something about the list bothered Natalie, but she couldn't think of what it was. Then it occurred to her. "All this stuff will get us started," she said. "What do we do when this stuff wears out?"

"We'll have to get our warm clothing the way people did for centuries before modern factories," Spider said.

"How is that?" Alexis asked.

Spider hesitated. "You're not going to like it."

"Tell me!" Alexis said.

"We'll have to hunt seals," Spider said. "Their skins will keep you warmer than anything else."

Natalie and Alexis looked at each other. Alexis said, "I guess I have a while to get used to the idea. I *am* a city girl."

"Not anymore," Spider pointed out.

Spider watched Alexis's expression as she thought about hunting seals, and he knew Cindy was right. Alexis was not as tough as she acted. She was downright squeamish about hunting and fishing. She'd always struck him as a little too serious, but now it occurred to him that anyone who genuinely liked rock climbing had plenty of fun in her. And anyone who cared that much about seals just plain had to be a good person.

"Besides," Alexis said, "it's not like we're going to kill a seal unless we absolutely have to. If we're cold and need the skin, we'll have to. At least on the island there'll be plenty of other food—if we get to the island."

"And the stuff we're going to buy will last for *years*," George said.

They were silent for a few minutes. Then Alexis said, "Hunting seals when we have to and living on a pure, pristine piece of land sounds a lot better to me than a federal prison."

"I agree," Spider said.

"Me, too," Natalie said. The very thought, though, of actually killing a seal made Natalie want to return to the world of *Middlemarch*. She pulled the novel from the bag and continued reading. In her peripheral vision she saw George, sitting next to her, take out *The Prince* and continue reading. When, some time later, he got to the end, he repeated, "Outrageous stuff!" Then he flipped back to the beginning, and started reading again.

9

They stopped for lunch at a rest stop just outside of Redding. To the side of the road were almond orchards. The sun was blazing hot. The sky was clear blue without a cloud anywhere.

The rest stop had toilet facilities and a row of picnic tables. Tammy selected a picnic table in the shade of a eucalyptus tree. The trees gave off a sticky, sweet scent. For lunch they ate various snacks they'd brought along. Tammy had a jug full of water, and a bag with groceries. She pulled out a loaf of wheat bread and a jar of peanut butter. They passed around the bread, a jar of peanut butter, and a plastic knife and made themselves sandwiches.

"Is the clock in your van right?" Cindy asked Tammy.

"Pretty much," she said. "Why?"

"I figured out the time and driving distance. We'll have to sleep somewhere along the road, or we'll get to the Canadian border in the middle of the night. Something tells me trying to cross at 2:00 a.m. may not be a good idea."

"Yup," Tammy said. "We will be much less

conspicuous if we cross the border in the morning. Where am I taking you?"

"When we cross the border I have to make a call," George said. "Then I'll know where we're going."

"I didn't hear that," Tammy said.

"Right," George said. "What you heard was me telling you we're going to a chess team retreat at the Riverside Cottage and RV Park on the Capilano River just outside Vancouver. We're meeting up with a Canadian chess team."

"Yes," Tammy said. "That was exactly what I heard. So what do I show them for paperwork at the border? I assume you brilliant kids have that figured out."

"You show them our letters from our parents allowing us international travel with the team in North America and Europe," George said, "and passports."

"Okay, I tell them you're going to a chess team retreat *where*?"

"Not just us," Cindy said. "*You're* going on the retreat, too. That's what we tell them. You and Veronica are the chaperones."

"Ha," Veronica said. "Dig me as a chaperone."

"So *where* is this retreat?" Tammy asked.

"The Riverside Cottage and RV Park on the Capilano River," Cindy said. "We'll write it all out so you can memorize it."

They finished their sandwiches and snacks, packed up, refilled water bottles from a drinking fountain, and used the restrooms.

They were back in the van when Cindy said, "There's a secondhand camping store in Redding. Can we make a stop there?"

"You kids need *camping* gear?" Tammy said.

"You're not asking questions, right?" George asked.

"Right," Tammy said. "I don't want to know a thing."

Evidently, though, Veronica did want to know a few things. She turned around and said, "*Camping?* For how long?"

Instead of answering, Alexis said, "I hope you like camping. We like it."

Veronica grunted and turned forward and looked out the window.

The secondhand camping gear shop was next door to a thrift store and not far from a discount department store. They visited all three stores, making purchases and crossing items off their list. From there, they asked directions to a garden store and a hardware store. It took two hours to get everything on the list, including four large secondhand duffel bags with wheels to carry all the stuff they bought. When they finished shopping, they had $325 left in cash.

The only place the duffel bags would fit was on the floor under their feet, making them feel even more squished. They settled back into the van and put their feet up on the duffel bags. Tammy turned on the radio and headed back to the highway. On the radio, the Eagles were singing about the Hotel California.

They rode in silence for a long time. Occasionally Liam leaned forward and talked to Tammy about the music. Mostly they read the books Cindy brought, or just stared out the window at the passing landscape.

Liam reached into Cindy's bag and pulled out a book. Natalie saw he was reading *The Complete Works of William Shakespeare*. She wondered which play he was reading. An hour or two later, when they were approaching Ashland, he replaced the volume of Shakespeare and took out *Classics of World Poetry*. He opened to a random page and started reading. She noticed, intrigued, that he often stayed on the same page for a long time.

By the time they approached Oregon, the terrain had entirely changed. No more scorched, dry, and brittle central California valley. Now the rolling hills were lush and green—a bright, tropical, citrusy green. Grass grew wild alongside the road. In California, you didn't see much grass unless people went to a lot of trouble to keep it watered.

They were just outside Ashland, Oregon, when Tammy stopped at a gas station. Alexis and George got out to help her with the pump.

Veronica turned around and said, "So how are we planning to live in Canada? In *tents*?"

They all looked at each other. Cindy said, "We don't think anyone should know where we're heading. Something may go wrong anyway. We'll tell you later."

"Tell me now," Veronica said. "I won't tell my aunt."

"We're not saying yet," Cindy said. "It's best this way."

Soon Alexis, George, and Tammy were back in the van, and they were on the highway again, listening to Led Zeppelin singing about the stairway to heaven. Natalie picked up *Middlemarch* and continued reading.

They stopped for a picnic dinner just outside of Eugene, Oregon. They didn't spend much time at the rest stop, though. They'd been snacking, so nobody was particularly hungry. They ate a little bit, stretched, used the restrooms, and climbed back into the van.

Before long, it started getting dark. Tammy said, "Time to find a place to stop for the night." She pulled off the highway onto a road that led into some woods. On both sides of the road were smallish deciduous trees and grass. She drove until she saw a dirt road leading into the brush.

"This doesn't look like it goes anywhere," she said. A short distance down the dirt road, she found a grassy area and pulled over.

Everyone got out of the van and stretched. They took turns wandering into the bushes. They were used to using nature for a toilet, after all.

Tammy popped open the top of the van, which created a bed. "Sorry, boys, you get the seats. The girls can squeeze up here with me. We'll be packed like sardines, but I think we'll fit."

Natalie didn't realize how deeply tired she was until she was in bed and closed her eyes. She hadn't expected to feel this weary after a day of driving on a highway, something she'd never done before. She concluded that running away was tiring. Even if sitting hour after hour in a van zooming north along Interstate 5 didn't *feel* tiring, just the thought of what you were doing was exhausting. Add to that the knowledge that after Monday they might be wanted by the FBI, and well, anyone would feel tired and stressed just thinking about it.

She would have liked to talk for a while with Alexis and Cindy, but with Tammy and Veronica in the bed, there just wasn't much they could say.

10

Natalie opened her eyes to the sound of birds chirping. She stretched herself awake. Weak sunlight streamed in through the windows. She lifted her head and looked around. The others were still sleeping.

Everything out here felt so different from San Francisco, even the feel and smell of the air. San Francisco was often damp, but this was a different kind of damp—warm and enveloping. The air smelled of pine needles and grass.

She slid to the foot of the bed, and lowered herself into the main part of the van. George was stretched across the front seat, sleeping. Spider was asleep on the rear seat. Liam was nowhere to be seen.

She grabbed her satchel and a bottle of water and slipped outside. Not far from the van, she found a private clump of bushes for a toilet and dressing room. She wanted to put on fresh underwear and a fresh tee shirt. She planned to wear the same jeans.

She was about to head back to the van when she heard the faint sound of a guitar coming from deeper in the woods. She walked toward the sound. In a small clearing she found Liam sitting on his jacket on a clump of grass, strumming his guitar.

Seeing her, he stopped playing and waved. She walked toward him, and sat on a fallen log about five feet from him.

"Play some more," she said. "I want to hear."

He strummed a few more chords, and said, "I was thinking we should write a letter to the world. Explaining what we did and why. If we get over the border, I mean. If not, we could be writing our letters from our prison cells."

"Yeah," she said. "A letter. *Dear World*. But how would we ever mail it without someone knowing where it came from? And who would we mail it to?"

He grinned. "Cindy will figure that out."

"I don't think the Robin Hood explanation will go over very well," Natalie said.

"Me neither." He played a few chords and sang:

> *This is my letter to the world,*
> *That never wrote to me,*
> *The simple truth that Nature told,*
> *With tender majesty.*
> *Her message is committed*
> *To hands I cannot see;*
> *For love of her, sweet countrymen,*
> *Judge tenderly of me!*

"What *amazing* lyrics!" She looked at him with astonishment and a new respect. "Did you write that?"

"No." He smiled and admitted, "Emily Dickinson

wrote it. But I *like* it. That's almost as good, right?"

"It's *totally* as good."

Seeing the admiration in Natalie's eyes made Liam's heart beat faster—and made him wish he *had* written it. He played some more chords. "I made up the melody, though."

"It's *beautiful!*" she said.

Just then, Alexis shouted from the direction of the van. "Everyone back! We gotta get going!"

Natalie and Liam walked back together. As they emerged from the woods, she caught the look on Spider's face. *It's not like that*, she wanted to tell him. But, of course, she couldn't. She didn't *really* know what he was thinking. More to the point, she didn't know how she felt, other than right now she was a little confused. And she was afraid life could become very complicated if she wasn't careful.

Everyone was busily packing up the van. The bed was already popped back down. When everything was packed, they all climbed into their seats.

"I'm a grouch until I get my morning coffee," Tammy said. She wheeled the van around, and headed back to the highway.

Spider sat quietly, watching out the window. The sight of Liam and Natalie emerging from the woods had set his temples pounding. He couldn't shake it off. For the second time in twenty-four hours, he felt a deep ache in his chest. He'd already gotten used to the fact that Natalie didn't want anything romantic to happen with him. He hadn't prepared himself for the possibility that she might want something romantic with someone else.

Cindy, sitting directly behind Spider, knew exactly what was happening. She'd seen Spider's expression when Natalie and Liam emerged from the woods. She saw the gloom settle on Spider. She sighed inwardly. Maybe her plan of distracting him with Alexis wasn't going to work.

They'd gone only a few miles down the highway when they came to a gas station with an accompanying market. Tammy pulled into the lot, parked directly in front of the store, and turned off the engine.

"I know for a fact," Tammy said, "that I'd better not attempt to cross a border with illegal minors and an adult jumping bail on a day that did not start out with a strong cup of coffee."

"I'll go with you," George said. To the others, he said, "I'll buy some food."

"Can you get a newspaper and a map?" Cindy asked George.

"Sure," he said.

The others stayed in the van and waited.

Soon Tammy returned with two paper cups of steaming coffee. She handed one to Veronica and put the other in the cup holder. George came out next with two grocery bags, which he passed around, and a newspaper and map folded under his arm. The first bag contained individual-sized plastic bottles of orange juice. The other contained two large bunches of bananas, a box of whole wheat crackers, and a package of mozzarella sticks.

George handed Cindy the newspaper.

Tammy leaned back in her seat. She took a drink of her coffee, and said, "Mmm." Then she sighed deeply and said, "I guess we should get going," but she didn't move to turn on the engine.

"I wrote this out for you," George said, handing Tammy a piece of paper. "Here's our story for when we get to the border."

Tammy turned and reached for the paper.

"But all you do is answer questions," George said. "Don't volunteer anything unless someone asks a specific question. Then only answer that question."

Tammy read aloud, "My niece and I are chaperoning these youngsters for a three-day retreat at the Riverside Cottage and RV Park on the Capilano River just outside Vancouver. The team will be meeting a chess team from Washington State, and a Canadian team—" She stopped reading and tucked the paper next to her on the seat. "All right," she said. "I can memorize this."

She put her cup into the holder mounted on the door, and started up the engine. She pulled out of her parking spot. Soon they were back on the highway, with Pink Floyd's "The Dark Side of the Moon" playing on the radio.

Cindy unfolded the newspaper and looked at the first page. Alexis and George, sitting on either side of her, looked also. There was nothing about the hacking on the first page. Cindy thumbed through each of the pages so they could read the headlines.

"The bank hacking isn't in here," Cindy said,

keeping her voice low enough so Veronica and Tammy couldn't hear.

"Maybe the bank wanted to keep it secret," George said. "Maybe they're afraid customers will panic if they know someone can hack in."

Natalie sighed and went back to *Middlemarch*. For some time—she didn't know how long—she lost herself in the novel. When she looked up again, all the others, including Spider, were reading—except Alexis, sitting directly to Natalie's right. Alexis sat staring straight ahead. "Pinball Wizard" was playing on the radio, with Tammy singing along.

Natalie put her book into her lap and looked at Alexis. "You okay?" she whispered.

"I'm nervous. How can you all sit there so calmly?"

Natalie didn't know the answer to that question. She shrugged to show that she had no idea.

"I'm worried," Alexis whispered. "Tammy did okay at the jail because the guy didn't ask her any questions, and because she could fake like she didn't know anything if she got caught. This is different. Veronica is jumping bail and trying to leave the country, and Tammy can't pretend like she doesn't know."

"Do you think she'll be able to get through the border?" Natalie asked.

"No, I don't," Alexis said firmly. "I don't think she can lie under pressure. If anyone starts asking questions, this could go very badly."

11

They passed a sign announcing the Canadian border in five miles. Tammy took the next exit, and swung into the parking lot of a mini-mart. "I need a little break before I can face those border officers. Anyone want anything?"

"I could use a restroom," Natalie said.

"Good idea," Cindy said. They all piled out, stretched, used the restrooms, and bought snacks.

After they returned to the van, Tammy sat in the driver's seat, but she didn't start the engine. She stared straight ahead. "I guess this is it," she said. "The moment of do or die."

"We'll get through," Spider said. "I know we will."

"What if we're searched?" Cindy asked. "Is there anything in here we don't want them to see?"

"The paper Tammy memorized?" Liam said.

"It's in the trash," Tammy said. "In the restroom in there." She gestured toward the gas station.

"Maybe we should let some of the camping gear show," Alexis suggested.

"Good idea," Spider said. He unzipped the duffel bag at his feet and pulled out two sleeping bags and a camping utensil set.

"Utensils," Veronica said, watching. "Speaking of utensils, I meant to give you all something." She reached into her purse, pulled out a metal object about the size of a stick of butter, turned around, and handed it to Liam, who was sitting just behind her.

"What's this?" he said, taking the object.

"A camping pocket knife," she said. "Top of the line. Has every kind of tool in there you need."

"Where did you get it?" Liam asked.

"The camping gear store," she said.

"Did you buy it?" Liam asked.

She shot him an amused look. "Of course not."

"See!" Tammy said. "I told you! Never let her into stores! You have to watch her all the time."

"I *was* watching her," Alexis said. "I watched her every minute we were in those stores!"

"Me, too," Natalie said.

"You must have blinked," Tammy said. "I am going to warn you all right now. This kind of thing gets worse when she isn't on medication."

"I just don't see how she did it," Alexis said. Good thing they were taking her far away from civilization.

"You know," Tammy said, "I'm feeling sort of nervous about crossing that border. Look." She held up her hands. "I'm shaking."

"Change of plans," George said, slapping his knees. "Veronica! Switch seats with me. I'll do the talking."

"That," Alexis said, "is a good idea."

Veronica and George both got out of the van. Veronica squeezed into the backseat between Natalie and the window. George slid into the passenger seat. Everyone gave George their passports and letters allowing them to travel.

"Veronica, why don't you give me your passport, too?" George suggested.

Veronica reached into her purse, fumbled in her wallet, then handed her passport to George.

Tammy started up the engine and pulled back onto the highway under the sign that said Interstate 5 North.

They passed a sign announcing Customs and Immigration ahead in a half mile. In the distance was a low cluster of buildings with a red and white Canadian flag flapping in the breeze overhead.

There were very few cars at the border crossing. Tammy selected the shortest lane.

George looked at Tammy. She seemed pale. "It's all right," he told her, and smiled. "Don't worry about anything."

"Yeah, right," she said.

The car in front of them, a green sedan, was stopped under the overhead. Tammy pulled up behind the car.

A youngish officer with thick brownish-blonde hair was at the window of the green sedan, talking to the driver. The sedan pulled forward and drove off.

Tammy inched forward and rolled down her window. When she came to a stop under the overhead, the officer stepped forward and leaned toward her window. "Welcome to Canada," he said. He looked in the van and said, "Camping?"

"Yes, sir," George said. "We're going for a three-day retreat at the Riverside Cottage and RV Park on the Capilano River."

He peered at George. He looked around at the others, then back at George. "Didn't I see you on the news? You were the kid asking everyone to send food and humanitarian aid to that new country in Asia!"

"Yup, that was me," George said. "We are very excited about this retreat. We heard great things about those cottages."

Cindy's heart thumped in her chest. Why hadn't it occurred to her that someone might recognize them?

"Paperwork please?" He looked at Tammy and said, "Passports?"

George opened the file, and handed him the letters and passports. Tammy reached into her handbag for her passport, and handed it to the officer.

The officer compared Tammy's and Veronica's pictures to their faces. Then he leafed through the letters. He handed everything back to Tammy. Tammy put her passport back into her purse and gave the remaining stack to George.

George saw that Tammy's hands were trembling. To distract the officer and keep him from noticing how nervous Tammy was, George shot him a smile and said, "Thank you, Officer! It looks like we're going to have great weather this weekend. We heard such good things about those cottages!"

"Can't do better," the officer said, "unless you head out to the island."

The mention of an island startled George—until he realized the officer meant Vancouver Island. George recovered, and said, "I hear it's nice out there, too."

"It's beautiful. You can get there by ferry."

"Sounds great!" George said.

The officer stood back and waved them through. "Have a nice visit."

Tammy drove forward. Once they were through the structure, she let out a deep sigh. She drove a few moments in silence, then turned to George, and said, "Young man, you have nerves of steel."

He smiled and shrugged. "Nothing to it."

"Except for the part about that officer recognizing you," Alexis said to George. "When the word goes out that we're missing, it won't be long before everyone will know we're in Canada."

"We are going to get caught," Veronica said. "I know it."

"We won't," George said. "Everything is under control. I have to make a phone call. Tammy, when you see a place to stop, would you mind?"

"Wait," Tammy said. "I thought you said no cell phones."

"I have a prepaid international phone," George said.

"How smart is that?" Tammy asked. "Looks like you kids thought of everything."

She took the next exit and turned onto a residential street. There were houses on one side and empty fields on the other. She parked to the side of the road near the fields.

George got out of the car and walked a short distance away. From his pocket, he took his prepaid phone and the card with Don's phone number.

He punched in Don's number. Don answered right away, his voice cheerful. "Hello?"

"Hey. It's me, George."

"George, buddy! How are you?"

"Not so good. I may be in some trouble."

"Trouble, huh? Well, I had a hunch this might happen. Big trouble?"

"Very big, I'm afraid. I'm calling from Canada."

"*Canada*? Are you *all six* in Canada?"

"Yup. We have Veronica with us, too. Remember her from the plane?"

"Of course I remember. Why do you have her with you?"

"It's a long story."

"Where in Canada?" Don seemed to be struggling to make the adjustment.

"Not too far from Vancouver."

"Any adults with you, other than Veronica?"

"Pretty soon it will be just us. You said if we ever need anything at all, we could give you a call. You said as a pilot you could probably get us aboard a plane if we needed to go somewhere."

"I did say that. And I meant it. I owe you all a whopper of a favor. I am assuming you have to hide because what you did with the Democratic Republic's website has gotten you into trouble with someone."

"Don, I hope you understand. I can't really say right now exactly why we're hiding. I hope later you don't feel I betrayed your trust."

"I said I owe you one, and I'm keeping my word. Where do you want to go?"

"Iceland. Then we want to try to get back to the island. If not *that* island—if it's too far from shore—a closer one, maybe. Where nobody will find us. We *could* just keep heading north from here, but we know how to live on that island."

What followed was silence. George realized he was holding his breath, waiting for Don's response. George considered how he'd respond if Don said, *No way, are you out of your mind?* or even *How do you expect me to get you back to that island? Do you think I'm a magician?*

What Don said was, "I'd have to rent a helicopter in Iceland to get you back out there. After what you did for me on the island, and what you did during the Asian nuclear crisis, I think I could rationalize it and justify myself. But what if something happens to one of you out there? What if one of you gets really sick, or hurt?"

"I can promise you this. Worse things would happen to us if we stayed."

There was silence. "You know I want to help you. I'm just not sure, George. It's a strange thing to say to a kid, but I believe you, and I believe in you. I just don't know about this."

George said, "If anyone ever figures out you helped us, you don't have to worry about being held responsible. If we get caught, and someone figures out you helped us, I intend to say that we blackmailed you, and you had no choice. After some of the things we've done, anyone would believe that."

Don sighed. "I'm not worried about myself. I'm worried about you."

"Will you help us?"

There was another long silence. "I'll do it, reluctantly, but I'll do it. I have to believe you're telling me the truth, that worse would happen if you didn't go. But I have a few conditions. Nothing you won't agree to, I'm sure. To begin with, I want you each to write letters to your families so they know you are okay. What phone are you using?"

"An international prepaid phone. Nothing can be traced."

"Give me an email address. In about a half hour I'll send you boarding passes. I trust you can talk your way through customs once you get to Iceland."

"Sure, no problem," George said. "I have to open a new email account so you can send me stuff. I'll call you back when I have it."

They said good-bye and disconnected. George put the phone back into his pocket.

He returned to the van. Veronica had moved back to the passenger seat, so he slid into the very back between Natalie and the window.

"Well?" Cindy asked.

"He'll do it," George said.

"He *will?*" Alexis asked, amazed.

"Yup," George said. "Now I need some Internet access."

"Peach's Internet and Gaming Cafe," Cindy said. "In Surrey, directly down Highway 99."

"Where is Highway 99?" Tammy asked.

"We're on it," Cindy said. "Interstate 5 turned to Highway 99 when we crossed the border."

Tammy started the engine, turned the van around, and headed back to the highway. She didn't put the radio on.

To the side of the road were grass and chain-link fencing. Beyond the fence were deciduous trees. The only clue that they were in Canada and not the United States was that the road signs were in kilometers and not miles, and a Canadian flag was flying over the "Welcome to Surrey" sign.

Peaches Internet and Gaming Cafe was on a side road in a mostly residential area set in a grassy field bordered by a row of tall skinny trees. There were a half dozen cars in the parking lot. Tammy parked toward the back of the parking lot, away from the building.

They all waited in the van while George went in. He was inside for about fifteen minutes, and then he came out through the door, blinking at the late morning sun. He got back into the van and said, "I didn't get the email yet that I'm expecting. I'll go in again in a few minutes."

The breeze was cool enough so that they were

comfortable waiting in the van. They were quiet as the minutes ticked by. Natalie took Alexis's arm for comfort. George appeared completely calm. After their first big win in California, when George finished giving a television interview, Natalie had asked him whether he ever felt nervous. "All the time!" he'd said cheerfully. "The trick is to fake like you're not."

Natalie had to hand it to him. If he was faking, he was pretty darned convincing.

After about ten minutes, George climbed out of the van and went back into the cafe. He wasn't inside long—no more than three or four minutes. When he came back out, he slid into his seat in the back, and said, "Tammy, if you could drop us off at the Vancouver International Airport, we'll be all set."

"Whoever's got a map, give me directions," she said as she started up the engine and headed back to Highway 99.

Cindy leaned forward and gave the directions. Vancouver International Airport was located about twenty miles northwest of Surrey. The drive took a half hour. The terrain was so flat that they could see the control tower and the Canadian flag flapping in the breeze from many miles away. The building was a modern glass and steel construction with a white overhanging roof.

"Does it matter where I drop you?" Tammy asked.

"Nope," George said. "Anywhere near a door. We'll be able to manage."

"So who did you call?" Tammy asked.

"I'd rather not say," George told her. "And you don't *really* want to know, do you?"

"You're right—I don't want to know." Then as she approached the terminal, she said, "Will you be able to send a postcard?"

"You'll hear from us," George said. "Don't worry."

Natalie shot him a look. She assumed this was true. He was a good liar, but he didn't lie to his friends.

Tammy pulled to a stop by the curb. Alongside the building was a row of old-fashioned pay phones. The glass doors leading into the building were the kind that slid open.

They all got out of the van and pulled out the duffel bags, backpacks, satchels, and Liam's guitar.

It's hard to say good-bye in a drop-off lane of an airport. Impatient drivers are honking, trying to get you to move. Security guards watch you suspiciously. But they did the best they could. They each gave Tammy a hug. Veronica and Tammy hugged for a long time.

"You take care of my niece, okay?" Tammy said. "And take care of each other."

"You know we will," Alexis said.

Someone behind honked to get Tammy to move along. She waved one last time, got back into the van, and drove away.

With the duffel bags on wheels and almost everything else in backpacks, satchels, or handbags, they were able to move easily into the terminal. Just inside the doors and to the right, they found a place without anyone around where they could gather and talk.

"So, dude," Liam said to George. "What's going on?"

"I had to open a new email account so Don could send me these." He took several sheets of folded paper from his wallet. "Boarding passes for Flight 379 to Iceland, with a stop in Montreal. Our flight leaves later this afternoon. It's a red-eye. We'll arrive at 9:00 a.m. local time."

"We're going to *Iceland*?" Veronica asked.

"We sure are," George said cheerfully.

"Don the *pilot* emailed you those?" Veronica asked.

"Yup," George said.

"How are we going to live in Iceland?" Veronica asked. "In tents?"

"We're planning to go back out to the island," George told her.

Veronica looked astonished. She looked around at each of them. "There's a lot you're not telling me. Right?"

"Not *too* much," George said.

"We should buy some more emergency food to take with us," Cindy said. "We can probably squeeze a few more things into our bags."

"That's right," Spider said. "Never get on an airplane without plenty of food. You never know when the avionics system might fail and you'll find yourself in the middle of nowhere."

12

The weather in Iceland was cool and drizzly, much like San Francisco in early summer. According to the announcement on the airplane as they landed, the temperature at the Keflavík International Airport was 58 degrees Fahrenheit.

They decided to separate as they went through customs. They suspected that the Canadian officer had recognized George because the news stories made a point of George being part of a chess team. But his passport said Xiuying Cheung, while the news reports referred to him as George, so they hoped if he was by himself nobody would recognize him.

Since George was the only one likely to run into trouble, they decided he should go through customs with Veronica. An adult with him would also make him less conspicuous. George and Veronica went first, and the others stayed toward the back of the line.

When Veronica and George reached the front of the line, Veronica handed the customs officer their passports and George's letter permitting international travel. The customs officer was a gray-haired man with a slight stoop to his back.

"How long will you be in Iceland?" the officer asked.

"Until tomorrow," Veronica said.

The officer looked over both passports, and said, "Welcome to Iceland." He stamped their passports and waved them through. George and Veronica went into the terminal and waited.

When the others reached the front of the line, the officer inspected their passports and letters. "How long will you be in Iceland?"

"Just one day," Spider said.

The officer looked up at Spider, then each of the others. "Where are your return plane tickets?"

"Our other chaperones have them," Spider said. "They are coming on a different flight."

The officer studied each of them, comparing their faces to their pictures. Alexis's heart was pounding so hard she felt dizzy.

Then the officer said, "All right, then." He stamped their passports and waved them through.

They met up inside the terminals and walked over to a quiet corner near a window.

"Whew," Alexis said. "We did it. Spider, you did great!"

"Thanks," Spider said. "Now that I know what a smooth liar I am, maybe *I* should go into politics."

"Ha ha," George said. "Very funny."

Alexis looked out the window. The skies were misty and gray.

Spider looked, also. "Looks just like home," he said. "Except for the grass, and the signs in Icelandic."

"It still doesn't seem real that we're here," Natalie said.

"How do you think *I* feel," Veronica said.

"I don't know!" Alexis said. "How *do* you feel?"

"Grateful, actually," Veronica said. "And still a little stunned. Are you ever going to tell me where you got the money to bail me out?"

"Certainly," Alexis said. "When we're on the island."

"Why do I have to wait? Do you think I'm going to *tell* someone?"

"No," Alexis said. "That just seems like the right time to tell you."

George took out the prepaid phone and called Don. Don said he was coming from France, and wouldn't arrive until about noon, Iceland time.

They chose to wait in a corner of the terminal away from the windows and away from the chairs. That way they could talk without being overheard, and they could sit back against the wall, or use their duffel bags for pillows and take a nap.

The terminal had that timeless and placeless airport quality. Some people were rushing by in a big hurry. Others were asleep in the chairs. Flight announcements came over a loudspeaker. The fact that none of them could understand a word just made the whole experience seem more surreal.

Cindy went to a counter and came back with a

map of the airport. "There are shops here," she said. "Who wants to come with me?"

"I will," George said. "Veronica stays here."

"Veronica will stay with me," Alexis said.

Natalie watched them leave. She was already feeling the jet lag. Her body thought it was 5:00 a.m. and that she'd been up all night.

Spider and Liam went off in search of food and came back with a tray of hot dogs.

"*Hot dogs?*" Alexis asked.

"Icelandic hot dogs are a delicacy," Spider told her.

Alexis raised her eyebrows.

"You'll see," Spider told her. "Try one."

She took a bite out of one of the hot dogs. Moments later, she was smiling. "*That's* something different," she said. "It *is* good."

Natalie took a few bites of a hot dog, but didn't feel hungry. The moment she put her head down on a duffel bag, she fell asleep. It was hard to stay awake when hit by jet lag. Soon they were all asleep—except Alexis, who had put herself in charge of Veronica, and felt someone should stay awake and keep watch.

* * *

Natalie opened her eyes and sat up. Spider and Liam were asleep by the wall. Alexis, Cindy, and George were huddled together, looking at a paperback with a shiny new cover. Veronica was near them.

"What are you looking at?" Natalie asked.

"A manual of plants in Iceland," Cindy said,

"including which plants are edible. We got it from one of the shops. We figure the island should have similar plants."

Natalie leaned forward and looked at the book. It was written in both Icelandic and English and called *The Hiker's Guide to Icelandic Plants*.

Just then, George's prepaid phone rang. He answered it, responded with a few "okays," then hung up, and said, "Don rented a van and is waiting in front of the baggage claim area."

They woke up Spider and Liam, and then lugged their stuff across the airport, following the signs to the baggage claim area. They went out the nearest door.

Don pulled up to the curb and they all climbed in.

Cindy sat in the passenger seat. "Thanks, Don," she said.

After all the doors were closed, he said, "It's the least I can do for the six kids who singlehandedly prevented a nuclear war. If I get in trouble, and nobody believes George's alibi for me, my defense will be that I couldn't say no to the kids who saved the world."

"*Excuse* me?" Veronica said. "You're joking, right?"

Cindy looked at Don and said, "Veronica doesn't know."

Veronica turned to Alexis, sitting next to her, her brows lifted in disbelief.

"I know it sounds preposterous," Alexis told her.

Veronica shook her head. "I guess it's no more

preposterous than a group of teenagers bailing me out of jail and then taking me to Iceland. Which raises a question. Why *here*? Why not a tropical island paradise?"

"This is better," Spider said. "No heat, no mosquitos, no diseases like malaria, plenty of fresh water. A hot spring. Salmon in the rivers and mussels at the beach. All you have to do is keep warm and you're all set."

"Yeah, that's all," Veronica said. "Just keep from freezing to death in the Arctic. What could be easier?"

"So what's the plan?" Cindy asked Don.

"I'm dropping you at a beach a few miles from here. I'll be back to pick you up in a helicopter in about an hour. The helicopter will be slower than the ones that rescued us. It will take about ninety minutes to get out to the island. I'll have to head right back."

"Thank you," Cindy said again.

"You have letters ready for me," Don said. "Right?"

"Here," Cindy said. She put an envelope on the dashboard. An email address was written across the front. "We wrote the letters on the plane from Canada."

"That's a thick envelope," Don said.

"We've each written to our families," she said. "There is also a general letter to the world."

"You wrote a letter to the world?" He sounded amused.

"It was my idea," Liam said. "You never know. Someone may actually read it."

"And how shall I deliver a letter to the world?"

"Do you know how to do blog posts?" Cindy asked.

"I'm sure I can figure it out," Don said.

"Good," Cindy said. "Post all the letters on a blog, including the letters to our families. That's my mother's email address." She pointed to the address on the envelope. "Open a new email account on a public computer with a totally made-up name, email my mother, give her the web address of the blog, and tell her to let the other families know. Then delete the email account."

Don considered this. "Smart," he said.

The road they were on took them due west, directly to the beach. Don drove along the beach for a mile or two.

"So, Don," George said. "What other conditions did you have?"

"I've given that some thought. I have written my own letter, which I've left in my locker in the airport in France. The letter is sealed, with the words 'open on my death,' on the front. I plan to put the letter in my safe deposit box. I am the only one who has the key. If I die or become incapacitated, my heirs will have access."

"What is in the letter?" George asked.

"Your whereabouts. Otherwise, if something happens to me, nobody in the world will know where you are. I can't have that."

George turned and looked at the others.

Alexis said, "Don, would you mind addressing that envelope to one of our parents, instead of just leaving it to your heirs?" She figured the letter should go to someone who wouldn't immediately tell the authorities where they were. She knew her parents wouldn't.

"I can do that," he said. "Be sure to write down the address for me."

Natalie, overcome with exhaustion, put her forehead against the glass and looked at the water. Don rounded a bend, then pulled over to the side of the road. Natalie could see right away that this stretch of beach was perfect—as deserted and remote as their island. They piled out with all their stuff.

"I'll be back shortly," Don told them, then drove away.

They lugged everything over to the sand. "This beach smells exactly like Mars," Spider said.

"I can't stay awake," Alexis said. "My eyes keep closing!"

"Have a nap!" Spider said. "Here, perfect place for a nap." He put the duffel bags together in the sand.

Alexis sat on the sand, leaned forward over the duffel bags, and promptly fell asleep.

She woke up to the thunder of a helicopter engine. Pulling her mind back through the fog of sleep was not easy. Spider helped her to her feet, and she brushed herself off.

A dark blue helicopter with a white stripe landed

about twenty feet from them, perched on metal legs. Don opened the door and motioned them over. "All of you, especially Spider!" he shouted. "Keep your head way down!"

They all ducked as they approached the helicopter, even though Spider was the only one tall enough to be in danger from the blades. The engine was roaring. They shoved all their stuff inside, then climbed in. Next to Don was a passenger seat. Behind him, two rows of three seats faced each other. In the back was a compartment that fit most of their stuff. The rest went on the floor under their feet.

George was the last in, so he sat in the seat next to Don. Once the doors were closed, the engines were less deafening. The sensation of the helicopter lifting straight up startled George, even though this time he was expecting it. From the air, Iceland appeared much larger than you'd think it would from looking at a map. As far as you could see to the east were mountains covered with rock and snow. A large city consisting mostly of low-lying buildings and houses stretched to the southeast.

Don turned some knobs and pressed some switches, and the helicopter sped off in a southwesterly direction. Just off shore were a number of small islands, some no larger than rocks jutting from the ocean. Behind them, the mainland grew smaller in the distance until it disappeared altogether and there was nothing around but ocean.

George didn't realize he'd fallen asleep with his

head back against the headrest until he felt the stomach-lurching feeling of the descent. He opened his eyes and leaned forward to look out the window, and there was Mars, spread out beneath them. He could see the jagged coastline, streams, and cliffs. There, nestled in the hills, was the hot spring.

The others, too, were waking up. They had all fallen asleep, including Veronica.

Don lowered the helicopter in the flat stretch of land near the airplane. Once the helicopter perched on the ground, he cut the engines and opened the door. The blades were still rotating, swishing above them.

"Keep your heads down," Don reminded them.

They unloaded their stuff and stepped to the ground. They looked and felt dazed.

"All right," Don said. "I'll be back in about a month, next time I'm in England. What do you want me to bring? What kind of food?"

"Chips Ahoy cookies for me," Spider said. "Real chocolate for those with classier taste."

"Books!" Cindy said.

"What kind of books?" Don asked.

"I brought mostly philosophy and literature," she said. "So how about politics, law, and history?"

Don raised his eyebrows. "You're an unusual girl."

"She openly embraces her nerdiness," Spider said.

George handed Don an envelope. "Here's all the money we have left." Don hesitated. George said, "Take it. There's nothing we can buy with it here.

Helicopter fuel is probably expensive."

Alexis handed him a piece of paper and said, "This is my parents' address. Address the envelope in your safe deposit box to them, okay?"

"That works," Don said. He gave each of them, including Veronica, a hug. Then he climbed back into the helicopter, started up the engines, and lifted up into the air.

All seven of them stood watching. As the helicopter moved farther from them, and silence settled around them, Spider said, "George? Aren't you going to make a speech?"

George cleared his throat. "Knights of the Square Table and Veronica," he said quietly. "Welcome home."

* * *

Don did not read the letters until he was back at the Keflavík International Airport in the pilots' lounge, sitting in a cushioned reclining chair. He opened the envelope and took out the letters. Each of the six had written letters to their families, assuring them that they were safe and happy, that they loved them all very much—and that they had good reasons for leaving.

The last letter was addressed to the world:

Dear World,

When things are so upside down that people who steal millions of dollars get rich, while a person who steals a dress goes to prison for fifteen years, and the kids who try to set things right are outlaws, well, there's isn't much anyone can do, right?

We would just like to tell you that we give up. There are just too many things wrong, like all those nuclear bombs, and all those homeless people while other people waste so much.

We tried to be modern-day Robin Hoods and fix some of the injustices, but we couldn't do it.

Meanwhile, we would greatly appreciate it if you would stop dumping toxins into the ocean, and if you would refrain from exploding any nuclear bombs.

Sincerely yours,

The Knights of the Square Table

13

"I have to quit soon," Alexis said. "I can't do much more."

"Yeah, I hear you," Liam said. "I am totally ready to drop."

"Me, too," Spider said. "I just want to use the rest of the mortar. Two more stones will do it."

Liam stood back to admire the wall they were building. "It's looking really good," he said.

The wall was now five feet long and seven feet high. Mixing the mortar, it turned out, was very hard work. Stirring the crushed and burned seashells with sand and water was so difficult they could do only a little bit at a time. It was easy to see why construction sites used concrete mixers. Finding the right size rocks and fitting them together were easy compared to mixing that stuff.

Digging the trench for the footing so the wall wouldn't shift was also hard work. They dug the trenches the same way they'd plowed their fields—in shifts. To call digging backbreaking work would be an understatement. At the end of each day they were all so sore they could hardly lift their arms. They had two shovels, so they took turns, two of them shoveling while the others rested. When it was your turn, you dug until you were too tired, and then you handed off the shovel and had a long rest until it was your turn again. It worked. In this manner they plowed two whole fields and dug the trenches for the walls.

They planned to build the wall twelve feet long and seven feet tall, and then add three more walls for a stone enclosure. Inside, they'd build a fireplace with a chimney. They planned to make a roof from heavy tarps, pitched steeply enough so that the rain and snow would run off.

They decided to build their village up in the hills, near the hot spring. It would be nice to be close to fresh, hot water all the time. For now they were sleeping by the plane, the girls in the cargo hold, the guys in sleeping bags around the fireplace.

It occurred to Liam that building a stone wall changed a person. After preventing a nuclear war, or even hacking into a bank, you *expect* to feel different. When you avert a war, you know you did something amazing. With a bank caper like they pulled, you might not be so sure what you did was *right*, but afterward, something about you is different, and not just because you're officially an outlaw. Something about you changes inside.

Building a wall, Liam realized, was like that, too. Afterward, you know you *can*. You know you can survive on a cold and remote island. You feel independent and powerful.

Liam watched as Spider spread the last of the mortar into place. Then Liam picked up a stone, and pressed it into the mortar, holding it until the cement hardened enough to hold it.

Just then Veronica came from around one of the hills, carrying a stone just the right size for the wall. She walked over and put it on the pile.

"Nice!" Alexis said. "Thanks!" Then: "We're stopping soon."

"That sounds good to me," Veronica said.

Some days, Veronica worked steadily right alongside the others. Even on the days she worked, she didn't say much, and when the day's work was done, she kept mostly to herself. Other days—in fact, sometimes for several days in a row—she didn't do much, just sat by herself, looking completely gloomy. During those times, they left her alone.

Spider spread the last of the mortar from the pan on the spot where the next stone would go. Alexis fit the stone into place.

"Done," Spider said. "Time for a hot bath."

"Let's go!" Alexis said.

The four who had been working on the wall—Alexis, Spider, Liam, and Veronica—grabbed towels and the extra set of clothes they'd brought from the plane, which they were using as a storage warehouse, and headed over to the hot spring. Spider was already anticipating the warm water. At the end of a day of work, there was nothing like sitting in the hot spring to soothe sore and tired muscles.

They no longer bothered to change into bathing

suits each time they went into the water. They bathed in underwear, then ducked into their makeshift dressing rooms, which they'd made by hanging a tarp between large rocks.

Alexis slipped out of her jeans and tee shirt and got into the water. She found a place to sit, and leaned back, putting her head back against one of the rocks.

Spider tried not to stare. He'd seen all the girls in their underwear often enough by now, but, well, a guy still liked to look, right? None of the girls wore anything lacy or revealing. Their underwear wasn't much different from a standard bikini, the bottoms a little thinner and clingier, but nothing you didn't see all the time on the beach. Still, it *was* underwear and it was hard to get used to seeing girls in it.

Alexis looked relaxed—and completely happy. Until they'd come back to the island, Spider had never seen her looking like this. She also laughed more. In fact, she laughed often, more than any of the others.

Spider lowered himself into the water and washed the tools they'd used—the pan they mixed the mortar in and the trowel they used for spreading it. When that was done, he found a rock to sit on.

"That's it for me," Liam said. He pulled himself out of the water and ducked behind the tarp to change clothes. When he emerged, dressed, he waved and headed down the hill. Spider knew exactly where he was going. He was heading for the plane, where he kept his guitar.

Veronica was sitting on the edge, dangling her feet in the water. Alexis was still submerged up to her neck, leaning back, her eyes closed. There was a hint of a smile on her face.

Spider had been paying attention ever since Cindy told him that Alexis secretly liked him, and sure enough, he saw the signs. He often caught her looking at him. He found it easy to make her laugh. She was also the only one willing to do any serious climbing or hiking. It was nice to have a companion as sturdy and eager for exercise as he was.

What he'd never really noticed—but what dawned on him one day shortly after they arrived—was that Alexis was really cute. She had finely chiseled features, a straight jawline, and a nicely shaped face. He hadn't noticed because she never acted cute and flirty, or walked in that self-conscious, deliberate way girls sometimes did when they knew you were watching. Not that Natalie did those things, but you couldn't miss Natalie's beauty. It hit you right away—that mass of dark curly hair, the big eyes, her tiny body that made you feel so much taller than you were. Alexis's good looks sort of crept up on you. He thought maybe he hadn't noticed before because she didn't used to smile much.

He also liked how she looked in a bathing suit, or in this case, her underwear. He liked it a lot.

He had by now completely given up on Natalie. He often saw her sitting by the fire with Liam, listening to him play the guitar. He knew she liked how Liam took poems from Cindy's book and put them to music. He had to admit that if music and poetry were her thing, he was probably not her guy.

Spider said, "You like it here, don't you?"

"I do, yeah," Alexis said, opening her eyes. "Strange, isn't it?"

"Not to me," he said. "I liked it from the beginning."

"Remember that morning back when we were stranded here," Alexis said, "and you, and me, and Liam went fishing? When we found the tide pool? You and Liam said you could stay here, forever, on this island. Well, let me tell you, I thought you were both completely nuts. I was furious when I realized we had to run away and come back. But I get it now."

"The only part I don't like," he said, "is the part about being here forever. It's kind of a long time."

"Yeah," she agreed. "A very long time. What about you, Veronica? Do you wish you could go back?"

"No," Veronica said firmly. "Not at all."

Spider wasn't surprised by her answer. He didn't know much about her life before they met her, but from the little he knew, he understood why she preferred being here. "See," he said, "camping's not so bad."

"It's better than jail," she said. "It's better than living on the street, which is where I was headed."

Alexis sighed. She leaned back again and closed her eyes. "We should get out and go find the others," she said, even though you could tell from her face that she didn't want to. The warm water felt so good.

Spider, too, leaned back and closed his eyes. He thought about how much they still had to do to prepare for winter. The thought gave him a feeling of something like anxiety—an entirely new emotion for him. Usually he was so carefree.

What helped were the length of the days. There was plenty of light for all the work that needed to be done. In fact, one of the hardest things to get used to about being on an island so far to the north was the length of the days. He didn't know exactly when the sun rose and set, but no matter how early he woke up, the sun was already up, and no matter how late he stayed up, the sun still hadn't set.

He understood that this was the summer they all had to be busy ants. If they played like grasshoppers, they'd be in trouble come January.

14

Usually Liam liked to play his guitar outside, near the fireplace. Today, though, he picked up his guitar from the place where he stored it in the plane and sat in the first row of seats, where he could stretch his legs forward. He practiced a new song he was composing. He was so absorbed in his music, strumming and picking the strings, that he didn't hear Natalie come in through the cargo hold. In fact, he didn't know she was there, in the seat across the aisle listening, until he glanced up.

When he looked up at her, she said, "That sounds nice. It's a new song, right?"

"Brand-new," he said, and continued playing, suddenly self-conscious.

He finished the piece, placed his hand on the strings, and looked at her.

"Can I try?" she asked.

"Sure! Have you ever played?"

"Never," she said. "The only musical instruments I've ever played were the harmonica and recorder. And I didn't play very well."

He handed her the guitar. She placed it on her lap

and leaned forward slightly, cradling the instrument. She strummed with her fingers, then smiled. "That sounded terrible."

"It wasn't bad," he said. "Here, I'll show you how to play a chord."

He moved to sit next to her, and showed her how to position her fingers to make the G chord. She didn't quite have the position correct. To show her how to do it, he moved her fingers into place. The moment he touched her, he felt a warmth shoot through his entire body. He glanced at her and saw that she, too, was suddenly flushed.

"Now hold your fingers steady," he said, "and strum with your other hand."

She tried it. "That sounds better," she said. She practiced strumming the chord several times.

"I'll show you another," he said. He showed her how to hold her fingers to make the C chord. She didn't quite have it right, so again he moved her fingers into place.

He had never been this close to her for this long, and he felt a little dizzy.

She strummed the guitar, playing the chord over and over.

"Now try going back and forth," he said. "First play one chord, then the other."

She tried it and said, "It's hard! It makes your fingers sore!"

"You just have to practice," he said.

She strummed a few more times. Then she handed him the guitar back. "I'll think I'll let you be the musician," she said, "and I'll just listen."

That was when they heard the droning of a helicopter. They looked at each other.

"Can that be Don already?" she asked.

"He said he'd be back in a month," Liam said. To keep track of the passing days, each morning Cindy put a pebble into a cup. He tried to remember how many were now, but he wasn't sure. "I'm sure it hasn't been a month," he said.

"Nope," she said. "It hasn't been more than three weeks."

She went to look out a window. "We'd better go see," she said.

They climbed out through the cargo hold. Cindy and George were already in the clearing, watching for the helicopter to appear. Minutes later, Spider and Alexis came running down the hill. Soon after, Veronica followed.

When the helicopter broke through the clouds, they could see it was dark blue with a white stripe.

"It's him!" Alexis said. Then: "I think."

"If it's not him," Spider said, "we're busted!"

"Don't say that!" Alexis said.

"I'm joking!" Spider said. "It has to be him!"

They stood watching as the helicopter landed. Liam, though, was lost in his own thoughts. He was thinking about what had just happened with Natalie—how she had blushed when he'd touched her. He wondered if she was encouraging him. He also wondered if he dared try to kiss her, should another such moment present itself. The very idea set his pulse racing.

The helicopter landed near the plane in a flat spot not far from where they'd planted their crops. The engines quieted, and the door opened. Don emerged, wearing his pilot's uniform. He ducked to avoid the blades, still swishing slowly, and walked toward them.

As soon as he was close enough, Alexis said, "You said a month! You scared me to death!"

"I came because I have some news that might interest you."

From the crinkle around his eyes and the glow in his face the news was obviously not bad.

He looked around. "Nice fields," he said. The tiny first sprouts were peeking from the earth. The plants consisted of a single stem and two leaves. There were rows and rows of them. "The place looks different! Show me around. I want to see what you've done."

"Tell us your news first!" Cindy said.

"I really want to see." He looked around. "Where are you living?"

"We're sleeping in the cargo hold and by the fire until we can finish building," Spider said. "We're building houses up on the hill, near the hot spring."

"That makes sense," Don said. "What are you building with?"

"We're starting with stone walls for a community shelter," Cindy said. "Did you know you can make cement out of burned seashells instead of limestone?"

"I didn't know that," Don said.

"After we finish the stone walls we plan to build individual sod-covered houses," Alexis said. "Like this!" She ran over to the cargo hold and came back with the drawing Natalie had brought.

Don studied the drawing. "This is really perfect."

"Now, please tell us the news!" Cindy said.

"All right," he said. "Which do you want first? The news, or your books and box of food?"

"Don, tell us the news!" Natalie cried.

"First I need to get something." He walked back to the helicopter. He reached inside and took out a large white envelope.

"Why don't we sit down?" he said.

"Over there!" Spider said, pointing to the stone fireplace they'd built not far from the opening to the cargo hold. They kept cushions just inside the cargo hold for anyone who wanted to sit around the fireplace. They pulled the cushions out now and arranged them around the fireplace so they could all sit comfortably.

Once all of them—including Veronica—were sitting in a circle, Don reached into the envelope and took out a sheet of paper.

"Let's start with this one," he said. "This article best summarizes what's been happening." He unfolded the paper and said, "I assume you all know something about a particular hacking job. Someone, *I wonder who*, hacked into the C&L bank system and stole about $400,000." He looked around at each of them. "Would anyone here know who that might have been?"

Alexis was astonished to realize Don was teasing them. He was treating the entire thing lightly, and she could not fathom why.

"Who would like to read this aloud?" Don asked, holding out the paper.

"I will," Cindy said. She reached for the paper. It was a printout from a network news website.

Don said, "You can start from the third paragraph down. The first two paragraphs describe the hacking, which I assume you already know all about."

Cindy skipped to the third paragraph and read aloud:

Authorities have concluded that the hackers were a group of ninth graders, San Francisco's all-star chess team. They call themselves the Knights of the Square Table. The group made the news in late March after being rescued from an island off the coast of Iceland. According to the pilot, the stranded passengers survived because of the ingenuity of the members of the chess team.

In hacking into the bank computer system, the youngsters' motive was evidently to seize the money they felt the bank had gotten through illegal and unfair bank fees, and redistribute the cash to homeless shelters and charities.

Cindy looked up. "Well, after the FBI showed up at Liam's house, we *knew* they'd figure out it was us."

Don looked at all of them. "So that's why you had to hide," he said. "It had nothing to do with hacking into the Democratic Republic's website."

Alexis watched Don carefully. His expression was relaxed.

"I'm surprised you're not mad at us for it," Alexis said.

"When I first read this, I was shocked. Your parents are being careful what they say in public, but I've seen them on the news and I can tell you that they are flipping out. But then, I was also shocked when I figured out what you'd done during the Asian missile crisis. I assumed you were on the run because of that, that somehow you'd gotten into trouble with someone for messing with the Democratic Republic website."

"No," Cindy said. "We're not hiding because of that."

"I'd think you would be *mad*," Alexis said. "Stopping a nuclear war is one thing. Hacking into a bank and redistributing the money is, well, a little more *controversial*."

"You can say that again," he said. To Cindy, he said, "Keep reading."

Cindy read:

> The revelation that the C&L hackers were members of the already famous youth chess team led authorities to a blog post evidently posted by the youngsters themselves shortly after they disappeared. In this blog post, they refer to themselves as modern-day Robin Hoods.
>
> The blog post has gone viral, inciting a storm of controversy. The ethics of what these youngsters have done is being widely debated on social media and talk shows.

Whereas initially the public reaction was shock and outrage, as of this morning, those defending their actions now outnumber those who criticize. Recent polls taken by the Central Broadcasting Network show that two in five Americans believe the youngsters should be brought to trial. In this shocking poll, three in five Americans are defending their behavior on the grounds that the banks should not have been allowed to keep the $30 million in unfair fees.

Cindy looked up. You could see she was stunned.

"I really didn't think the Robin Hood explanation would fly," Natalie said.

"Me, neither," Alexis said. "I have a hard time believing people *approve*. What's going to happen now? Is everyone going to become outlaws and start hacking into banks? Good-bye, law and order."

"These numbers *sound* great," George said, "until you realize that an awful lot of people out there want to put us in prison!"

"These numbers *are* great, George," Spider said. "We're more popular than the president of the United States. With these numbers, your career in politics may not be over after all!"

"There's more," Don said. "Keep reading. You haven't gotten to the good part yet."

Cindy continued reading:

The C&L thus found itself at the center of a raging controversy. Whereas most Americans had been unaware of the bank-fees scandal, the controversy has put all the facts in the public eye for a full week.

In what may have been a move to put an end to so much negative publicity, C&L asked that charges not be pressed against the young hackers. The Board of Directors has unanimously voted to make gifts of the money that has been distributed.

Cindy looked up. "They're letting the homeless shelters and food banks keep the money?"

"Yup," Don said. "Keep reading."

Cindy read:

A member of the C&L legal team said, "We do not believe the bank fees were unfair or illegal, but we understand that the public perception is that they were. Therefore, in a gesture of good will, we have decided to match the donations. We will donate an additional $400,000 to homeless shelters, food banks, prison reform organizations, and organizations working toward world peace."

After Cindy read that last line, her jaw literally fell open. She looked around at the others. The only sound was the cawing of a flock of seagulls overhead.

Natalie was the first to speak. "That's a lot of money! Think of all that money for charity!"

"It's still a small part of the illegal fees the bank executives kept," Cindy said, recovering. "And it helps. But throwing money at a problem doesn't solve it. It offers some relief for all those poor people, but the whole system has to change so there isn't any more poverty and homelessness."

"Cindy?" Don said. You could hear the amazement in his voice. "Do you have an idea for how to do that?"

"Not yet," Cindy admitted.

He gave her a look that was hard to read. One of his eyebrows was cocked.

He reached into the envelope and took out another piece of paper. "Here's the other news. First, you need to know about a few changes in the past two weeks. The Democratic Republic held elections to transition from a temporary military government to a more stable one. The guy we've all been referring to as the dictator won by a landslide. He's now known as the president of the Democratic Republic. He's very popular with the people there." He handed Cindy the paper and said, "Now read that one."

She read aloud:

> The government of the Democratic Republic has confirmed rumors that on the final day of the missile crisis, hackers entered the Democratic Republic government website. Sources within the Democratic Republic confirm that on that same day, the president of the Republic took a phone call from a youngster who was later identified as Xiuying Cheung, known as George, one of the C&L hackers and one of the passengers stranded for a week on Flight 690. This is the same young man who later that day took to the airwaves,

encouraging the world to send humanitarian relief to the Democratic Republic.

Authorities believe George Cheung and the other hackers were looking for the president's personal contact information. While nobody knows exactly what was said during the eleven-minute phone call, the president confirmed that the young man was persuasive and convinced him to come to the negotiating table.

George Cheung and his fellow teammates were last seen crossing the Canadian border at Surrey, British Columbia. They are believed to be hiding on the Canadian coast.

Don looked at George. "What *did* you say to the president of the Democratic Republic?"

"I'd rather not tell you," George said smoothly. "It would be like giving away trade secrets."

Don looked around at the others. His eyebrow was again cocked. He shot Veronica a questioning look.

"I don't even know," Veronica said. "They're keeping it to themselves."

"All right," Don said. "There's one more article I want you to read. George, I think maybe you should read this one." He handed George an article torn out of a newspaper. George read:

George Cheung has become a folk hero in the Democratic Republic. The citizens of the new country credit Mr. Cheung, age 15, with providing the large influx of food and humanitarian aid that brought so many of its citizens from the brink of starvation. His picture can be seen posted throughout the Republic.

"You really are famous, George," Liam said.

"Oh, yes," Don said. "World famous. You're *all* famous. Your 'Dear World' letter had already gone viral when the Democratic Republic story broke. As of yesterday, *millions* of people shared your blog post, and millions more retweeted it. The blog post is being shared on Facebook and reprinted in newspapers. The post has received more than two *billion* hits, setting a new record for hits in a single week. Jacy Skye's latest release has half that number."

He went back into the helicopter and came back with a box. "I printed out all the comments on your blog. There are tens of thousands."

"The comments on our blog post fill *that* box?" Natalie asked. The box was big enough to hold ten reams of paper.

"I also included a few thousand of the comments from Twitter. Figuring out how Twitter works was not easy. How do you kids *get* these things? I put as many tweets as I could on each sheet of paper. Eleven point font, single-spaced, printed on two sides."

"It's all such a shock," Natalie said. "I don't even know what to think of all this."

"What it means," Don said, "is that you can go home. You don't have to worry about prison. If the bank doesn't want you prosecuted, you probably won't be."

This was met with silence. The Knights of the Square Table looked at each other.

"*Probably* doesn't mean we *won't*," Alexis said. "It's still pretty risky. Forty percent of the people out there want us in prison. And we can't *all* go home. Veronica jumped bail."

"Don't worry about me," Veronica said. She turned to Alexis, but she was talking to all six of them. "If you all want to go home, I understand."

"But what *about* you?" Alexis asked.

Veronica stood up. "This isn't about me right now." She turned and climbed into the plane through the cargo hold. She slid the panel closed.

"What has she been like?" Don asked quietly.

"Great, actually," Natalie said. "Some days she works as much as any of us. She keeps to herself, but she talks to me sometimes."

"I'm sure she'd like to go back, if she could, right?" Don asked.

"I don't think so," Natalie said. "She doesn't have any reason to go back. Things weren't so good for her."

"I feel badly for her," Don said. "And I probably sound calloused when I say this, but you kids have to do what's right for you. As she said, this isn't about her."

"Can we have a chance to talk about this?" Cindy asked Don.

"Of course," he said, "but I don't know what

there is to talk about. You can't stay here forever."

"We really don't want to risk prison," George said.

"You think risking jail time is worse than being stranded on an island in the middle of the ocean?" Don asked.

"Yeah, actually, we do," Alexis said.

There was silence. Then Liam said, "I'm not going to prison, Don."

"I know you did great for the ten days we were here," Don said. "And you're obviously doing well now. But you could starve here."

"We won't!" Spider said.

"You honestly thought I would leave six kids on a subarctic island all winter?" Don asked.

"You'll have to," George said. "Unless you plan to turn us in, and we hope you won't."

"I really think you should reconsider," Don said. "I think you should go home."

* * *

While the Knights of the Square Table had a meeting to vote on what to do, Veronica gave Don a more complete tour. She showed him the potato fields they'd plowed. If all went well, the three large jars full of seed potatoes they'd gotten from the garden store in Redding should yield them 450 pounds of potatoes. Next season, they'd get more. They planted their potatoes near a cluster of wild berry bushes because they figured the soil there was good. They'd already planted kale, their winter crop.

She took him up the hill to the place they had chosen for their village. He inspected the stone wall. "They really do intend to stay, don't they?" Don asked.

"We all do."

* * *

Meanwhile the Knights of the Square Table sat in a circle around the fireplace.

"I'm not sure about going back," Alexis said. "Plenty of people still want to put us in jail. Why take a chance on that when we can be here?"

"I don't understand how we *wouldn't* be arrested for hacking into a bank," Natalie said. "I don't think Don understands how horrible prison would be."

"Yeah," Liam said. "It's a lot of work being here, but there's something I really like about it. I feel like—who was that dude who went to the woods to live deliberately?"

"Henry David Thoreau," Cindy said. "He also went to jail for doing something that he thought was right."

"I guess we should vote," Natalie said.

All six voted to stay. They wrote the next letter for their blog:

> *Dear World,*
>   *So, it looks like you approve of our actions. You've made us stars. You admire what we've done.*
>   *Well, we don't believe you. What we are is a fad. We're trending on Twitter, but something else*

will trend tomorrow. We're a momentary diversion, a nice idea.

Tomorrow you will have forgotten about us and moved on to the next Twitter sensation, and nothing will have changed. There will still be twenty thousand nuclear bombs. There will still be people who waste too, and then step over homeless people in the streets. There will still be people spending fifteen years in prison for stealing dresses while bank executives get rich through unfair fees.

Meanwhile, we are building ourselves a lovely little utopia, and we intend to stay here.

We want a simpler life—a life in touch with the real world, the world that matters, the world you are destroying. We are here to live deliberately.

If you mean what you say, that you admire what we have done, you will stop building prisons and bombs, and you will build hospitals and schools instead. Do you really need twenty thousand nuclear bombs?

Sincerely,
The Knights of the Square Table

15

Breakfast included fresh berries. According to *The Hiker's Guide to Icelandic Plants*, the berries were not only edible, but nutritious as well. They were blue— not the blueberries they were familiar with but sweet and delicious.

They ate their breakfast sitting in a circle on cushions around the fireplace.

"You know," Natalie said, "being international celebrities doesn't really change much, does it? We still do the same things we did before."

"Not much changed on the outside," Liam said. "It just all *feels* different. Especially after reading those tweets and blog comments."

There were so many blog comments and tweets in the box Don left for them that they'd divided up the printouts and reported back to the group on anything particularly interesting they found.

Marissa, Natalie's sister, had posted, *Natalie! Where are you! Please, please call me!*

Other family members had left carefully worded comments telling them to come home as soon as they could.

There were, as Don said, many who thought the Knights of the Square Table should be hunted down, arrested, and imprisoned. The haters, Liam called them. The haters accused them of setting a bad example, advocating anarchy, and championing the wrong causes. Among the names the haters called them were wrongheaded and silly-minded. And there was much worse.

They also had defenders. Lots of defenders.

The two most memorable tweets were by Brad King, a well-known movie star, and Jacy Skye.

Brad King had tweeted, *They are messiahs, prophets, leaders, and rebels.*

Jacy Skye had tweeted, *It's all too late, they say. There's nothing left to do.* Liam said her tweet sounded like the start of a song.

"I like being an international celebrity," Natalie said. "Even if it doesn't change much."

"Yeah," Cindy said, "me, too. Maybe this was why we called ourselves the Knights of the Square Table. Maybe we knew all along that we were going to turn into defenders of peace and justice."

"Better be careful," Liam told her. "The Knights of the Round Table didn't end up so well."

"Fill me in," George said. "I don't know the story."

"The knights wanted to create a perfect community called Camelot," Liam said. "They came up with slogans like 'might for right.' They vowed to defend the defenseless."

"They couldn't do it?" George asked.

"They came close," Liam said. "But Camelot was destroyed by uncontrolled human passions and jealousy. The queen fell in love with Sir Lancelot. The king found out. And from there, it was all downhill."

"Nothing like that is going to happen to us," Natalie said firmly.

* * *

It was up to Natalie, she knew, to keep their little community from being destroyed by jealousy.

When they finished their breakfast and each put their dishes into the pot of water for washing, Natalie avoided looking at Liam. She usually avoided looking at him when others, especially Spider, were around.

"We need some more seaweed," Alexis said. "And maybe crabs for lunch."

Spider sprang to his feet. "When is low tide?" he asked.

Liam looked for the moon. "A little while."

"All right," Alexis said. "Let's work on the wall till then."

At first, Natalie had been surprised by Alexis's eagerness for climbing, gathering, and exploring. She'd also been surprised—and very pleased—that Spider and Alexis had taken to each other. The more she thought about it, though, the more sense it made.

Sometimes things just work out just the way they should.

Because Alexis and Spider so often went off exploring together, Natalie felt freer to sit with Liam by the fire and listen to his music, which she absolutely loved. She felt completely at ease with Liam, who was quiet and inward. She liked his music and his poetry, which she felt gave her a glimpse into what he was really made of.

Nobody knew how she felt—not even Liam—and she intended to keep it that way. She hadn't asked for another guitar lesson because she knew what would happen. The pleasure she had felt when he'd touched her hands had startled her deeply. *This was how it's supposed to be*, she'd thought to herself. She knew if she got that close to him again, he'd kiss her, and then everything would change, and she just wasn't ready. Not yet. She'd made up her mind that nothing romantic was going to happen between her and Liam until she was completely confident that Spider longer no cared.

Their little community would *not* be torn apart by human passions and jealousy.

16

Each time Don came, they gave him another letter for their blog, and he brought a box of comments, responses, and tweets. They were, unbelievably enough, having a conversation with the world—or a lot of it, anyway.

It was a midmorning in late August when they heard the distant drone of a helicopter. Liam, Alexis, and Spider were putting the tarp roof onto the community shelter. Natalie, George, and Cindy were hilling the potato plants. Veronica was gathering large stones for the last wall.

Natalie was the first to see the helicopter. "It's Don!" she shouted.

Liam, Alexis, and Spider must have run all the way down the hill because they arrived just as Don was landing in the clearing near the airplane.

"How many days has it been?" Liam asked.

"Thirty," Cindy said. "So he's right on time."

No matter how many times Cindy heard it, she could not get used to the roar of a helicopter. Ordinarily the island was quiet, with only the sound of the sea, the cawing of seagulls, the wind, and at times the falling of rain. After the usual silence, the roar of the helicopter was unpleasant and even disturbing.

Cindy stepped back with the others to watch as Don landed. The helicopter seemed to hover for a few seconds, like a humming bird, before descending straight down and alighting gently on the spindly legs.

Don turned off the engines and opened the door. The blades slowed and made a rhythmic swishing sound like a heartbeat.

When he stepped from the helicopter, Natalie thought he seemed relaxed and happy, but that might have been because he was dressed in casual clothes—jeans, heavy shoes suitable for hiking, a tee shirt. He looked entirely different.

"This time," Don told them, "the news I have for you will make you *want* to go home. At least I hope so."

"Tell us!" Cindy said.

"First I want to see what you've done." He walked over to the field and looked over the rows of potato plants. They were now grown large and bushy. It would not be long before they'd be ready to harvest potatoes. Beyond the potatoes were rows of carrots and onions. Planted among the potatoes were beans. Don bent to look closely at the potato plants in the first row.

"These look good," he said. "You're going to have quite a harvest."

"We hope so," Liam said.

"Okay," Cindy said. "Now tell us the news!"

Don walked over to the helicopter, reached inside, and took out a box so large he could hardly carry it. The box was about twice as large as last time, big enough to hold a small refrigerator.

"Let me help you with that!" Spider said.

"Let's carry it over there," Don said.

Spider and Don lugged the box over to the circle of cushions around the fireplace near the cargo hold. After they were all sitting down, Don patted the box and said, "The fad, if that's what you are, is showing no signs of going away. I've printed out all the blog comments and relevant tweets and articles. This should keep you reading for a while. It's filled with stuff about you."

"So we're still famous," Spider said.

"Even more so," Don said. "Your families started a petition, which has been signed by hundreds of thousands of people. It went to the California governor and United States Department of Justice, asking for any charges to be dropped against all of you, so you can return home. They also asked for immunity for anyone who is hiding you, who I suppose in this case means me."

"That's great!" George said.

"There was a lot of discussion," Don said. "Lots of people felt you should have to face *some* consequences. There was talk of forcing you to make restitution, but that was difficult since you didn't keep any of the money. So all you have to do is publicly promise that you will not do any more hacking."

He paused for emphasis, and then said, "The California governor and the United States attorney general have signed the promise of immunity. So you can go home. All of you. Even Veronica."

"Me?" Veronica said. "I guess they figured out we're all together."

"Yes," Don said. "That wasn't hard."

"Wait," Alexis said. "Let me see if I understand this. We are pardoned for using stolen money to bail Veronica out? She's pardoned for jumping bail? All we have to do is promise not to do it again? How can that be?"

"You're not *pardoned*," Don said. "A pardon is what happens after you're convicted. In this case, the state of California and US attorney general agree not to bring any charges against any of you. In fact, the bank doesn't want you prosecuted. The last thing the bank wants is more publicity over those fees. Of course, you have to promise not do any more hacking. You have to give your word."

Spider laughed out loud. "That's funny! Taking the word of a bunch of outlaws!"

"You'd have to stop hacking," Don said. "Of course."

"What if we can't?" Cindy asked. "What if we have uncontrollable urges and impulses to set the world right? What if we can't bear injustice and unfairness or fighting, and when we see it, we feel we have to intervene?"

"You'll just have to learn to control that," Don said.

"Look," Alexis said, "I'm glad we all get immunity. Especially you, Don. I'd hate for you to get in trouble for helping us. And it's not like I want people after me trying to put me in jail or anything, but it doesn't seem right that we'd get away with everything we did while others have to go to prison for things not even as bad as using stolen money for bail."

"Alexis has some interesting ideas about prisons," Spider told Don. "She wants there to be community service, education, and mental hospitals. She thinks we have too many prisons and too many prisoners. She thinks a lot of the people in prison shouldn't be there."

"How does a teenager *get* these ideas?" Don asked.

"I've always been kind of opinionated," Alexis said.

"Okay, my young opinionated friend," Don said. "What punishment do you propose for someone like Veronica, who steals something?"

"She has to give it back!" Alexis said. "What's the big deal? You can't punish her into not being mentally ill! Besides, punishing mentally ill people probably makes them crazier!"

Natalie glanced at Veronica to see how she was responding to this. Veronica was hiding a smile. When Veronica realized Natalie was watching her, she said, "It makes a lot of sense, doesn't it? That's what I like about Alexis. She makes sense."

"What about people who steal, but they're not

crazy?" Don asked.

"You mean like the bank executives?" Alexis said. "They should have to give it all back! They shouldn't get to keep any! They shouldn't be able to get rich from unfair fees!"

Spider cleared his throat. "Excuse me, Don. I advise you not to argue with Alexis. You won't win."

Don laughed. "That's very good advice. And I think I will follow it. So will you all go home now? You were running because you were in trouble for the C&L hacking, right? And for bailing Veronica out with stolen money, taking her across the border, et cetera. Now you're not in trouble anymore."

For a moment, the only sound was the cawing of seagulls in the distance.

Then George said, "That was part of it. But not all of it. Once we started looking, we felt bothered by things we saw."

"Hmm," Don said. "Just like the new Jacy Skye song."

Liam sat forward. "She has a new song? It's probably no good. Her music was becoming self-absorbed and stale."

"I brought a recording," Don said, "so you can decide for yourself."

He took a music-playing device out of his pocket. He pushed the play button, and held it up so they could all hear. The music had that familiar, folksy Jacy Skye sound with an up-tempo beat. When she sang, though, her voice had a new depth and passion:

It's all too late, they say,
There is nothing left to do.
They made a little peace on earth
But could not see it through.
Hey, hey, hey.

To hold fast to their humanity
They've gone to live deliberately
And build their own utopia.
Hey, hey, hey.

It's all too late, they say.
We can only fall.
Coulds, and shoulds, and Robin Hoods,
The children in us all.

After a few more repetitions of the last line, the music faded out. Listening, Natalie felt something tug inside, that stirring that happens when you listen to something beautiful. It was the same feeling she got listening to Liam's music. She stole a glance at Liam and saw that he, too, was deeply moved.

Liam was the first to speak. "She wrote a song about *us*?"

"It looks that way," Don said.

"What do you think of it, Liam?" Natalie asked him quietly.

"Amazing," he said. "It's a real departure for her. I'd like to hear it again."

So Don played the song again. They listened once more through until the music faded into silence.

"So what are you doing?" Don asked. "Going home, right?"

This was met with silence. You could see Don was surprised—or perhaps puzzled—by their reaction.

"Can we have some time to talk about it?" George asked him.

"Certainly," Don said. "Take all the time you need. If you don't mind, I'd like to stay for your discussion. I understand you have secrets you're guarding, but if you don't trust me now, when are you going to trust me?"

They looked at each other. "I agree with that," Natalie said. "I'm fine with Don staying for our meeting." The only secret they were keeping at that point was that they'd essentially blackmailed the president of the Democratic Republic into coming to the negotiating table, and they were accustomed to keeping that from Veronica.

"I'm fine with it, too," George said.

The others nodded and agreed. Don could stay.

17

The problem was that nobody said anything. And the silence had nothing to do with Don being there. Natalie glanced at Liam. He looked back at her. She didn't have to ask how he felt. She knew. He liked it here. He liked having a community of people around him. He also liked being with her. At the same time, he was also practical enough—and smart enough—to understand that staying forever meant hardship and deprivation. Even Spider, who was fine with a lifetime of hunting seal and living off the land, didn't really want to cut all ties with his family forever.

Suddenly Cindy said, "I'd like a little time to myself before we talk about it."

"Why not?" George said. He was watching her carefully. He was pretty sure he knew what was going on with her.

She stood up, sighed deeply, and said to the group, "Look, I *do* know it's all my fault that we're here."

"You need to stop saying that," Liam said. "We keep telling you it isn't your fault."

"We're all glad we did it," Natalie told her. "We're glad we stopped that war. We're glad we redistributed the money. So are a lot of people out there."

"I know," Cindy said, "but I still feel responsible for getting us all into trouble." She turned and crawled into the cargo hold, then climbed into the plane. George knew she was going to the front of the plane, which they'd converted into a library. The pilot and copilot seats were plush and comfortable. That was where he and Cindy sat and read, and talked about books. It was a good place to be quiet and contemplative, sitting in comfy seats with the windows open on all sides.

"Why does she think it's her fault?" Don asked.

"It was her idea to try to do something about the Asian missile crisis," George said. "The hacking wasn't her idea, though. We stumbled on that while we were trying to figure out what to do. The second hacking was really Spider's idea, but everyone thought he was joking."

"I *was* joking," Spider said. "But here we are." He grinned. "Which just goes to show, you better be careful what you joke about."

"I just don't understand," Don said. "If you can go home, why not? All you have to do is not break any more laws."

"What would Robin Hood have done if you told him to stop stealing from the rich?" George asked.

"I also think she doesn't want to be the holdout vote," Natalie said. She turned to Don and said, "All important decisions have to be unanimous."

"Speaking of that," Veronica said, "when the voting starts, I'm going to leave. I am not going to vote."

"But you need to tell us what you want to do," Natalie said.

"Not as long as decisions have to be unanimous," Veronica said. "There's no way *I* will be the holdout vote."

"If we vote to go home," Natalie asked her, "you'll go with us, right?"

"I don't want to be part of the discussion," Veronica said. "At all. I don't want anything about me to be part of the decision." She stood up. "I'm going up to the hot spring."

They watched as she walked away. Once she was out of earshot, Don said, "You don't think we can get her to come?"

"I don't think so," Alexis said.

"So she would just stay here, on the island?" Don asked. "She'd die."

"Eventually, yeah," Alexis said. "But I get how she feels. If I knew I'd just end up living on the streets of a city or sitting in a prison, I'd want to stay here, too."

"That makes things difficult," Don said. "We can't very well leave her here."

That was when Cindy emerged from the plane

and sat back down with the others. "Where's Veronica?" she asked.

"She doesn't want to vote," Alexis said.

Cindy absorbed this, then said, "All right, what do you guys think?"

"What do *you* think?" George asked her.

"I think going home at the center of so much positive attention is a good way to go back," Cindy said. "We might be able to use all that celebrity to do good things. But I think we'll end up back in the same place. At least I will. I'll start feeling frustrated that I can't do anything to solve the big problems. And then I'll get another crazy idea."

"And I've put my foot down," Alexis said. "No more crazy ideas." She hesitated and added, "Unless it's for another really, really good cause."

"But I don't want to be the one to make everyone stay," Cindy said, "if you all want to go home."

"That's it," Spider said, slapping his knee. "I'm going to make this easy for everyone. I vote to stay, at least for a little while longer. Now nobody has to worry about being the holdout vote. I'll do it. I'm not ready to go back. We just spent months building stone walls and plowing potato fields with two shovels. I want to eat those potatoes. I want to use the room we built."

"Well," George said, "I guess that pretty much solves it, at least for now. We can't go back." He grinned and said, "We'll wait until Cindy thinks she can control her criminal impulses."

"I guess we need to write another letter for the blog," Natalie said. "We still accept the offer of immunity, right? We can promise not to do any more hacking. If we stay here, there's no danger of breaking our promise."

They all agreed.

"You write your letter," Don said. "Then I will fly back to the mainland and post it. I can use the computer in the pilots' lounge at the airport. I'm retired now, but nobody will care if I go in. But then, if you all don't mind, I'd like to come back and stay for a little while. I took out the helicopter for two weeks. I said I want to go on an extended fishing trip."

"Two weeks!" Natalie said. "Did you know this would happen?"

"I had no idea what was going to happen. There are too many things I just didn't understand. But I came prepared. So, can I stay for a few weeks?"

"Of course you can stay!" Natalie said. The others nodded and said, "Yes! Of course!"

"You don't mind camping?" Liam asked.

"I love camping. Here's a little-known fact about me. I was quite the backpacker in college. In fact, I hiked hundreds of miles along the Appalachian Trail. I'm also quite the fisherman." He turned to Spider and said, "I have fishing poles in that helicopter that I think you're going to like."

"You're really going to join us?" Spider was grinning. You could hear in his tone that he was flat amazed.

"There is something appealing about what you kids are doing—living off the grid, building your own community, living a simple life. Not having to turn on the TV or browse the Internet for all that bad news will be a relief."

"Living off the grid," Natalie said. "I never heard that phrase before. I like it."

* * *

Liam drafted both letters, and passed them around to the others for suggestions. They sat together on cushions in a circle not far from the airplane and tinkered with the wording. When they were finished, the first letter looked like this:

> *Dear US Attorney General and California Governor,*
>
> *Thank you for your generous offer. We gratefully accept your offer of immunity, and we promise not to do any more hacking.*
>
> *Sincerely,*
> *The Knights of the Square Table*

And the second letter looked like this:

> *Dear World,*
>
> *Thank you, family and friends, for petitioning for us to get immunity. We love you very much, and we feel very relieved—even though we don't think it's fair to people inside the prisons, who aren't famous*

and who don't have families who can do what you did.

It's nice to know we can come home if we want to.

Here's what's stopping us: We got into this mess because we wanted to solve all the big problems in the world, but we didn't see any legal way to do it. There are still some big problems we want to solve. For example, there are still twenty thousand nuclear bombs in the world, and some countries are still trying to build more. Living under the threat of nuclear war is just too horrible. There are other problems, like pollution in the oceans and air, and people wasting too much, and too many poor and hungry and homeless people.

We see no way to solve these problems, and we find that frustrating.

Also, we like it here. We like building our own community. When you build your own community, you can make everything perfect.

So for now we want to stay here, where life is simple and beautiful and we are not causing any harm, and we can live just the way we want to.

Sincerely,

The Knights of the Square Table

P.S. This is to Marissa, from Natalie: I don't think you really want to join us. It's awfully hard to live where we are.

Natalie read the letter over once more. "Something is still missing," she said.

"What?" Cindy asked.

"I'm thinking," Natalie said. She wrinkled her brows and had that intent look of concentration she often got in a chess game. At last, she said, "I think I know what's missing from that letter. We need a question of some kind. We've closed and locked the door. We need to open it a little bit."

"What do you mean?" George asked.

"We need another P.S." Natalie reached for the letter. Liam handed her the letter and his pen. She added this to the letter:

> *P.P.S. Now that you all understand why we can't come back*—*we want to solve the problems but we have no legal way to do it*—*does anyone have an idea? Something we can do other than live off the grid and build our own private utopia? We will read your comments.*

18

Don pulled a bunch of wicker chairs from the helicopter. "I know what kind of equipment a serious fisherman needs," he said. Each day, Spider and Don—and anyone else who happened to feel like fishing—sat in the chairs by the stream with their lines dangling into the water. Often, like today, Don and Spider were there long after the others left. It was now late in the afternoon, but the sun was still well above the horizon.

"You kids had the right idea," Don said. "If you have to hide from the law, this is a good place to do it."

Spider grinned. "Careful, Don. Before you know it, you may want your own little sod house."

That was when Spider felt a tugging on his line. He stood up and got a good look at the fish. "It isn't too big. It's not shrimpy either." The fish was about six inches long, big enough to be worth cooking and eating, but not big enough to put up much of a fight. He easily reeled it in.

Once the fish was in the bucket with the others, Don stood up. "That should do it," he said. "Don't you think?"

"Yup," Spider said. "We have more than enough."

They folded the chairs, and carried the rods, the bucket of fish, and the chairs up the hill.

The others were at the hot spring, sitting on rocks, dangling their legs in the water. Don and Spider waved, and put the bucket of fish inside the stone room near the fireplace.

Spider and Don found a place for themselves on the rocks, removed their shoes and socks, rolled up their pants, and dangled their feet in the warm water.

The others were talking about Jean-Jacques Rousseau's *The Social Contract*, a book about political philosophy. Cindy insisted that they all keep reading and learning even though they weren't in school. She preferred books about how to set up a perfect society. Spider listened, but didn't participate much in the conversation. He was impressed that all the others, including Liam, had read the book closely enough to be able to discuss it intelligently. Spider figured he just wasn't the philosophical type.

Once they all grew quiet, Don asked, "Tomorrow is a rest day, right?"

When a few of the others nodded and said, "Uh-huh," he said, "Then I think I'll fly back to the mainland tomorrow. Check my email, check your blog. My two weeks with the helicopter is just about up."

"Already?" Natalie asked. "Time goes fast, doesn't it?"

"You know," Don said, "I was thinking. As long as you're all staying here, I think I'd like to stay with you. I'll have to do a few things before I come back. Like put my house up for sale. Since my wife died, I've been meaning to sell it. It's too big for just me. I'll take out a long-term lease on a helicopter."

"You know you're welcome here, Don," Spider said. "It will be great to have you."

The others agreed.

"It will take me at least a few weeks to get back," Don said. "Maybe longer."

19

George and Cindy were sitting together in the cockpit. Cindy was reading, but George wasn't. He was staring out the window, not thinking about anything in particular. He felt bone tired from all the work that day. Besides, sometimes he found reading with Cindy sort of unnerving, the way she flipped the pages so quickly, then had almost total recall of everything she read.

When the drone of a helicopter came from the distance, they looked at each other.

"He said at least a few weeks," George said. "It hasn't been that long, has it?"

"It's been nine days," she said. "I'll bet something's up." She put a scrap of paper into her book for a bookmark. "Let's go," she said.

By the time the helicopter came into sight, breaking through the low-hanging clouds, the others had gathered in the clearing. They watched as Don landed the helicopter not far from their fields. The blades were still rotating, making their swish-swish noises, when Don stepped down from the helicopter, ducking. He reached back into the helicopter and took out a cardboard box.

He walked toward them. Once he was close enough, George said, "Hey! You're early!"

"And why do you think that might be?" he asked.

"You have news," George said.

"I do," Don said. "Let's sit over there." He gestured to the cushions in a circle around the fireplace near the plane.

Spider and Liam carried the box for him. Once they were all sitting down, Don took a newspaper from the box and handed it to Cindy, who was sitting closest to him.

"Open to the first full page," he told her.

Cindy opened the paper, and there was a full-page ad, directed to them. The headline was: "Dear Knights of the Square Table."

"That ad," Don said, "appeared in all the major newspapers of the world, and is being tweeted online. That P.P.S. you added, asking for suggestions, has brought some interesting responses, as you'll see when you read through your blog comments. This ad is easily the most interesting."

Cindy looked closely at the page, then looked up at the others. "It's a message to us," she said, "from an organization called Nations United for Peace." She grinned. "They want *us* to be consultants and spokespeople."

"*Seriously?*" Alexis asked.

"Yup," Don said.

"I never heard of the Nations United for Peace," Cindy said.

"It's new," Don said. "The people who formed the organization were inspired by what the six of you did during the Asian missile crisis. They decided the existing organizations had become too political. They just weren't making progress. So this organization formed. More than a hundred nations have joined."

"Did the United States join?" Cindy asked.

"Yes," Don said. "Almost immediately."

"What about the Democratic Republic?" Cindy asked.

"Not yet. The president of the Democratic Republic issued a statement that he'd be willing to join if a certain young man who calls himself a Friend of the Planet Earth, otherwise known as George Cheung, will take on the role of mediator."

"He wants *me*?" George said. He looked around at the others.

"Why are you so surprised?" Don asked. "What *did* you say to him during that conversation?"

"I still think it's best if we don't tell you," George said.

"They still won't tell me, either," Veronica told Don.

"I *assume* the president of the Democratic Republic wants George because his television pleas made George a national hero in the Democratic Republic," Don said. "And evidently George made quite an impression on the president during that conversation."

"Is this a joke?" George asked. "Or a trick?"

"Of course not," Don said. "They want the kind

of publicity you'll bring. *Everyone* is reading your blog and discussing your letters and what you've done. Someone is even writing an opera about you. What you've done has really captured the world imagination. Averting a war is not something most people are able to do. So I really hope that now you'll consider going home."

"Can we have a few minutes to talk about it?" George asked.

"Certainly," Don said. "Do you mind if I stay again?"

"Fine with me," George said. The others nodded and shrugged.

Natalie handed the newspaper to Liam, who read it and passed it along. After they'd all had a chance to read the ad, and absorb what it meant, Cindy said, "I think people will listen to us now. I think if we handle this right, we won't be a passing fad. I think we *can* do some good. Without breaking laws."

"The only problem is," Spider said, "I'm really not ready to go home. I mean, I miss my family and all, but I like it here, too."

"Yeah," Alexis said. "Me, too."

"There's always a compromise," Natalie said. "What if we accept the offer on the condition that we can live here? Why not, right? How hard would it be it for us to install some way to communicate? It doesn't take long to get to Iceland by helicopter, and Iceland isn't far from the European continent. Why not ask for permission to base ourselves here? We have immunity, so we can go home anytime to visit, or we can invite people here. We can ask permission to call the island ours."

"That," Cindy said, "is a brilliant idea."

"Except for the part about our parents having fits," Spider said.

"We'll have to reason with them," Alexis said. "I think they'll get it. I think the idea will work. The ad says they'll offer us payment."

"We don't need much," Natalie said. "Payment for our services could consist of use of a helicopter to come and go from the island whenever we want, and a small stipend for buying supplies."

"Do you think they'll agree?" George asked.

"All we can do is ask," Natalie said.

George looked at Don and asked, "If they agree, do you mind flying us back and forth?"

"Of course not," Don said. "It's the least I can do in the interests of nuclear disarmament and world peace."

"All right then," Liam said. "Let's write the letter."

So they did. This was what they came up with:

Dear Nations United for Peace,

    We would be proud and honored to serve as consultants and spokespeople for your organization. We believe that it should be possible for all the countries of the world to live together in harmony, and we will do all we can to help bring this about.

    Your ad promises payment for our services. We are now living on an island hundreds of miles from any country. When we arrived, the island was uninhabited. We believe this island is uncharted and not owned by anyone.

In exchange for our services, we would like to call this island home. For payment, we ask for use of a helicopter so we can return when our work is finished. We have a pilot here who can fly the helicopter. We imagine dividing our time between living here on this island and working with your organization and visiting our families. We would also like a small stipend for supplies—but we need very little.

We will wait for your reply.
Yours truly,
The Knights of the Square Table

"All right then," Don said, "I'll go post this on your blog. I'll come back when there's a response."

* * *

Don was back the very next day with this response:

Dear Knights of the Square Table,

We are happy to agree to your conditions. We will designate a helicopter for your use and offer a stipend of $1,000 per month. Will that be sufficient?

If you agree, we would like to begin by meeting all six of you at our headquarters in Switzerland. We will then provide transportation for a visit to California so you can visit your families before

beginning your work with our organization.
    Yours truly,
    Denise Williams
    Executive Director, Nations United for Peace

The six Knights of the Square Table gathered around Cindy, who read the response aloud. Then they passed the paper around so they could each read it.

Cindy started to speak, but stopped. She wanted to say, *it was Natalie's idea to ask the question in our letter,* but she felt too overcome for words. Everyone watched her, waiting for what she was about to say.

She looked helplessly at George.

George cleared his throat. Not quite sure what he was going to say, he began with, "Ladies and gentlemen, members of the San Francisco all-star chess team." He paused. Then, it came to him. "Now it's up to us."

20

Cindy stepped into the helicopter, feeling trembly and excited. Now that they no longer had to hide their whereabouts, they were off to Iceland to call their families. Veronica had refused to come. "Who am I going to call?" Veronica had demanded. "My aunt? My cousins? I think my aunt Tammy already told you they've all written me off." Alexis offered to call Tammy for her. Veronica had responded that it didn't matter to her.

When Cindy and the other five Knights of the Square Table stepped into the helicopter that morning, all six of them carried their tablets and telephones. Don had a charger in the helicopter for their batteries.

Don started up the engine, and they lifted into the air. Cindy looked down. What she liked best about landing on or taking off from the island was being suspended in the air and seeing the entire island at once. Veronica was still standing where they'd left her in the clearing not far from the plane, looking up at them, waving.

Even from up here, the rows and rows of crops

they'd planted were impressive, as was the stone room they'd built not far from the hot spring. She saw steam rising from the pool of water.

Cindy was feeling particularly eager to call her parents. Unlike, say, Alexis's parents and Spider's parents, hers had been more cryptic in their blog post messages. They didn't write as much and their tone was harder to read. But that was the way they were. Like Cindy, they were reserved, particularly with strangers and particularly in public.

Her mother was a librarian, but not the friendly sort who sat at the desk and cheerfully answered questions. She had the back-office job of ordering books and deciding which books were not circulating enough to earn their place on the shelves. Her father, too, had a quiet job. He did scheduling for the Muni transit system, spending most of his day working with a spreadsheet. Even her sister, off at college, was studying to be an accountant, a profession that didn't require her to be outgoing and friendly. Her brother, Mark, was the only family member not shy with strangers.

The last time Alexis's parents had posted to the blog post, they'd written, "You're in this far, Alexis. You may as well see it through." Spider's parents, in an interview, had said, "We were shocked at first by what he'd done. But now that we understand it, we don't feel we should stand in his way or try to stop him." Cindy's parents hadn't said anything like that.

The island was no longer in sight. All Cindy could see in every direction was ocean.

"I'll admit something," Natalie said. "I'm excited about calling home." In fact, the mere thought of it put a flutter in her stomach. She hadn't realized how much she missed her family until now, when it looked like she'd be able to go back for a visit. Mostly, she missed her sister Marissa. The only time she ever felt at all homesick was just before she fell asleep—the time she was used to telling Marissa goodnight.

Natalie knew from the happy flush on Cindy's cheeks that Cindy was feeling the same way.

"Is anyone tempted to *stay* home?" Alexis said. "Now that we can?"

"I am certainly not tempted," Cindy said. "We have important work to do. I don't see how we can do it from home."

"We can't," George said. "We won't accomplish anything without publicity. If we go home, and go back to being ordinary high schoolers, eventually we'll stop being media sensations and there will go all our publicity opportunities."

Natalie caught the look that crossed Liam's face. He was skeptical, she knew, about whether in fact they would be able to do any good. He'd mentioned to her that none of them really knew what the Nations United for Peace expected from them. They were supposed to be consultants and spokespeople— but what did that *really* mean? They knew from the newspapers Don brought back with him that trouble was brewing again in Asia. The situation was probably much more complicated than any of them realized.

"I'm surprised your parents aren't going to try to force you all to stay home," Don said. "You're *kids*."

"Did you know," Cindy asked, "that in the middle ages, by the age of fifteen most people were married with children? Fifteen-year-olds were considered adults. An extended childhood, and even the designation of teenage years as part of childhood, is a relatively new idea."

Don smiled. He tended to smile whenever Cindy talked like an encyclopedia. "I didn't know that," Don said. "When *my* son was finishing ninth grade, he was *not* acting like an adult, I can assure you of that. I don't know what I would have done if he'd been involved in some of the things you kids have done."

"Don, you would have been *great*," Alexis said. "Just like you're being now."

"I agree," Cindy told Don. "If your son thought he could bring about world peace, would you have stood in his way?"

"That isn't the question," Don said. "The question is what I would have done if my son had wanted to run off and live on an island when he was your age. And I believe I would have said no."

"That's because your son wasn't a Knight of the Square Table," Alexis told him.

Don smiled. They rode the rest of the way in silence. When they approached Iceland, Don flew low along the beach. He picked a stretch of sand close enough to Reykjavík so they'd get telephone reception, but far away from roads and trails so they were unlikely to meet up with any people. He found the perfect place, a stretch of beach cut off on all sides by mounds of rocks and cliffs.

Don landed the helicopter, turned off the engine, and opened the door. They all climbed out.

Cindy wandered off and checked to make sure she had reception. She did. The signal was weak, but strong enough for a phone call. She dialed her mother's phone number.

Her mother answered on the first ring. "Cindy!" she said.

The emotion in her mother's voice brought tears to Cindy's eyes.

"Hi, Mom."

"Hold on, let me call your father!" Cindy heard shouting and some commotion in the background.

"Cindy, are you there?" her father asked. She could tell from the echo that she was on speakerphone.

"Yes, I'm here!"

"Where are you?" her mother asked.

"I'm in Iceland to make a phone call. We have no reception—"

"You need to come home," her father said sternly.

"We *are*—" Cindy said. She was about to say they were coming home for a visit after meeting with the executives of the Nations United for Peace, but she stopped because she understood that her father meant come home *and stay*.

Cindy had trouble speaking. She'd never gone against her parents before—at least not openly. "Dad," she said quietly, "I don't think you understand this opportunity. The Nations United for Peace want *us* to be spokespeople and consultants."

"You can do it from home," her mother said.

"But I can't," Cindy said. "How will I fly back and forth from California to Switzerland? It's so much closer from here."

"I said no," her mother said. "You need to come back. We got you immunity, Cindy. We can't keep bailing you out of trouble."

"You won't have to," Cindy said quietly. "I promise. We're not going to get into any more trouble."

"We will see you soon," her father said.

They said good-bye, and she disconnected and walked back to the helicopter. The others were spread out over the beach. Alexis was closest to the helicopter. She could see from how broadly Alexis was smiling that she was having a very different kind of conversation.

Cindy heard Alexis say, "That's *so* nice of Liam's parents!" Alexis was silent for a while, listening, and then she said, "It's *like* we're in school! Cindy has us reading books." She laughed and said, "Political philosophy!"

Alexis was silent for a moment, listening, and then she repeated, "Yup, philosophy!" Then: "All right Mom, Dad! I gotta go! See you soon! I have to make one more phone call!"

Alexis hung up, scrolled through her contacts for another number, then put the phone to her ear. "Hi!" Alexis said. She listened for a moment, then said, "We're in Iceland! . . . No, we're not living here. We're living on the island. It's great. We're building houses and—"

Alexis listened for a few more minutes, then said, "You *do*? Okay, I'll ask the others. Talk to you later! Bye!"

Alexis disconnected and walked back to the helicopter. When they all finished their conversations and gathered together, Cindy asked Alexis, "What did Liam's parents do?"

"They want to install a communication system on the island," Alexis said.

"Yup," Liam said. "That's what they just told me. They know someone who is a wizard with communications systems who can help us get the whole thing installed."

"That's great," Cindy said.

"So everything's okay?" George asked, speaking to all of them.

Everyone, including Cindy, nodded. She wasn't ready yet to talk about the conversation she'd just had. The only person—other than herself, of course—who was not wearing a happy smile was George. She wondered if his parents had a reaction similar to hers.

Don asked, "What's next?"

"We can get on the Internet from here, right?" Cindy asked. "We may as well see what's new."

Liam turned on his tablet and opened an Internet browser. First he went to a major news website. Natalie, who didn't have Internet access on her phone, stood nearby to read with him. The others read the news on their phone apps. There was now a refugee crisis—thousands of people, including children and elderly people, who either had left what was now the Democratic Republic, or were forced to leave during the fighting that had brought the current president into power. The refugees were homeless and living in temporary camps. Many claimed to be enemies of the new Democratic Republic, swearing to bring about its downfall.

Some of the refugees had left to form an army to try to take back the country. Others had fled because they were frightened. The Democratic Republic refused to let any of the refugees back because they had no way of knowing which were enemies of the new government and which were not.

"It's always something," Don said wearily. "There is always unrest or war somewhere on earth."

"There shouldn't be," Cindy said firmly. "There doesn't have to be."

Liam next went to their blog. There were 3,532 new comments—way too many to read standing there on the beach beside the helicopter. "I'll download all these comments on my tablet," he said, "so we can read them later."

When that was done, he did a Google search for "Knights of the Square Table," and hundreds of pages of hits came up.

"I still can't get used to being famous," Natalie said.

"I don't think I'll ever get used to it," Liam said.

Liam clicked on some of the entries, and glanced at a few of the articles and commentary. Most of it was positive, but there were still haters who accused them of being criminals and setting a bad example.

"I'll call Denise Williams now," George said.

He used his own cell phone. The others listened to his side of the conversation. Mostly he just made sounds of agreement: "Okay . . . uh-huh. . . that's great, thanks . . ."

When he hung up, he said, "She wants us to arrive at the Keflavík International Airport Monday at 8:00 am. She'll have tickets arranged for our flight to Switzerland. She thinks reporters will be trying to talk to us, so she'll ask a security officer to escort us to our plane."

Next they checked their personal email accounts, and each of them spent some time sending email to relatives and friends. Cindy didn't have much email. Unlike George, she had a very small circle of friends. George, on the other hand, had almost one hundred personal emails. Most of them he downloaded to read later.

Later, when they were back in the helicopter, heading toward the island, Alexis said, "Veronica's aunt Tammy wants to come, too."

"She *does*?" Cindy asked.

"Yup," Alexis said. "She asked if she can. She was amazed when she learned we're living on the island."

Natalie said, "My sister Marissa really wants to join us here. Can she?"

"I don't see why she can't come," Spider said. "Does she like camping?"

"She's never been camping, except for a fifth-grade overnight field trip. But I think she'll like it."

"Are your parents going to let her?" Cindy asked.

"It looks like it. She's seventeen. She told them she'll take care of me." Natalie laughed a little at that. "Besides, they think it's just until we do whatever we need to do to help the Nations United for Peace."

21

Cindy didn't say anything to the others until the evening before their trip to Switzerland. They'd finished a dinner of salmon and potatoes, and were all sitting with Veronica and Don around the fire not far from the opening to the cargo hold. The evening was drizzly and damp, so they had mounted tarps overhead to keep themselves—and the fire—dry. The wind kept causing the fire to flicker.

That was when Cindy said, "I'm not going back to California. You'll all have to go without me."

"Really?" George asked. "Are you sure?"

"Very sure, yes," Cindy said.

"That makes two of us," George said.

George and Cindy exchanged sympathetic glances.

"Why didn't either of you say anything before?" Alexis demanded.

"I just needed to think about it," Cindy said. "My parents surprised me." She looked at George and said, "What did yours say?"

"I just don't think they get it," George said. "I'll call them again when we're in Switzerland. I'll invite them to come visit, if they want to. But I am afraid if I go back, they'll order me to stay."

"Same here," Cindy said.

"What if they order you home?" Natalie asked.

"I'll tell them that I *will* go home," George said. Then he added, "Eventually."

Spider laughed out loud. "Spoken like a true politician."

Cindy was glad nobody asked any other questions. She felt hurt, and a little embarrassed, that her parents just didn't get it. She wondered if the Nations United for Peace would withdraw their offer if they knew her parents were opposed to her staying.

"About tomorrow," George said. "I don't think we have the right clothes for a meeting with executives. I didn't bring a tie."

"A *tie*!" Spider said. "I don't even own a tie. I've never owned a tie." Spider looked down at what he was wearing. "All right. Our usual clothes might not give off the right image. But this is as fancy as I get."

"Yeah," Alexis said. "Me, too. Just try to make me wear dressed-up uncomfortable shoes."

"I'm with you on that one," Spider said.

"I think our clothes are okay," Natalie said. "We washed everything."

"I think so, too," Alexis said. Then: "Wanna know what I'm most looking forward to about visiting home?"

"A bed with a pillow?" Don asked.

"Nope," Alexis said. "A washing machine and dryer."

* * *

"Look at that!" George said the next morning as they descended toward the Keflavík International Airport. There were hundreds of reporters, all held back behind a rope. "I didn't expect so many."

"Yikes," Cindy said. "You're doing the talking, George."

"Yup!" George said. "No problem."

Don landed smoothly and easily where the air traffic controllers directed him. Once they were on the ground, Don opened the door. No sooner had they emerged from the helicopter when the reporters started shouting questions at them. Cameras flashed.

A uniformed airport security officer came to greet them. "Welcome," he said. "Follow me."

To get to their plane, they had to walk past the reporters.

George walked up ahead with the security officer. The others followed behind. George went right up to the rope and greeted the reporters.

One of the reporters leaned toward George, holding a microphone. "So you've been hiding on the same island where you were stranded?" she asked.

"We have, yes," George said.

Cindy noticed that reporters often asked questions when they already knew the answers—the sort of thing dull teachers did.

"When you removed $400,000 from that bank," another reporter asked, "were you at all tempted to keep *some* of the money?"

"Of course not," George said. "Now we'd better

go. We don't want to miss our plane."

"One more question, please!" asked a reporter, a young man with an accent Cindy didn't recognize. He was wearing a tweed jacket and a beret. He pushed past the other reporters until he was by the rope.

"Certainly," George said to him. "This will be the last."

"The missile was lowered at approximately 4:50 Eastern Standard Time," the reporter said. "Your phone call to the president occurred approximately 90 minutes later. Your phone call, then, could not have been what convinced the president to lower the missile. Can you please explain?"

Cindy felt her knees go weak. George, however, didn't miss a beat. He took one more step forward so he could speak clearly into the microphone.

"Now you know the truth," George said. His voice had such depth, and he spoke with such authority that Cindy felt certain he was about to confess that they'd lowered the missile and then blackmailed the president.

What George said was: "The president of the Democratic Republic is honorable and peace-loving. He had already decided to try to bring about peace by the time I spoke to him on the phone."

"What, then, did you and he *talk* about?" asked the reporter.

"We had a *very* interesting conversation," George said. "About the need for peace in the region, how oppressed his people were feeling because of the sanctions, how he felt pushed by the entire world toward a war that he didn't want." George paused again for drama and said, "We really felt a connection."

Cindy smiled. She couldn't help herself. She felt such relief she had to hold back a giggle. Thank God George could lie so easily and smoothly.

It was only later she realized that while George had given a smooth lie that would further his hero status in the Democratic Republic and help his relationship with the president, it was not likely to be well-received by the refugees.

22

The Knights of the Square Table met with Denise Williams and six other executives and directors of the newly formed Nations United for Peace in a small conference room of a Geneva hotel. They sat in deeply cushioned chairs around an oval table covered with a white cloth. The room had wood-beam ceilings and stone walls painted a creamy vanilla white. On the table were glasses and pitchers of ice water and orange juice. There had been a light rain that morning. The windows were open, and from the street came the smell of warm asphalt.

All six of them listened as Denise told them about the latest development in Asia. They listened attentively, even though they had already read the latest news on the plane. In fact, Cindy had placed the newspaper she'd brought—one of the major American papers—on the table in front of her.

The story about the refugee crisis was buried on the fifth page with a small headline. What made the whole thing odd was that a story about *them*, the Knights of the Square Table, was on the front page, along with a sports story, a local election story, and a story about the rising cost of health care in the United States.

The news, buried there on the fifth page, was distressing. Apparently each side had captured a key leader. The refugees, who were gathering and training an army with the aim of toppling the president and new regime, had captured a leader of the Democratic Republic who went by the name of Cai. The Democratic Republic had captured a leader of the refugees' new army, a general who went by the name of Ja-Long, meaning Like a Dragon.

Cindy put up her hand as if she were in class. Denise smiled at her and said, "Yes, Cindy?" the way a teacher might.

"Would you mind if I do some research while you're talking?" Cindy asked shyly. "I'll be listening."

"Go right ahead," Denise said.

Cindy began clicking on her telephone. George scooted a little closer to her while trying not to be obvious about it. He wanted to see what she was reading. She had opened her Google app, and was searching for information about Ja-Long. After skimming quickly through several articles, she did a Google search for Cai.

Meanwhile, Denise continued talking about how sensitive the situation was: Both sides refused a prisoner exchange because each considered the prisoner they held to be too important to the other side. Now both sides were threatening to execute their prisoners. If both men, Ja-Long and Cai, were executed, there would be uproar and violence.

Suddenly Cindy sat up so straight in her chair everyone looked at her. When Cindy realized Denise had stopped talking and everyone was watching her, her cheeks turned pink. Everyone waited, expecting her to say something. So, quietly, she said, "Did you know that Cai is the nephew of the president of the Democratic Republic?"

"I *did* know that," Denise said. "I entirely forgot to mention it. He's really a grandnephew, the son of the president's niece."

"He's very well educated," Cindy said. "He's trained as a soldier, but he went to college in Beijing."

Another of the directors in the room, a man with gray hair and glasses, said, "Both men are well educated. They both went to college in Beijing, so they both speak Mandarin as a second language. Perhaps coincidentally, both men went to the same university. They have much in common, but of course, their politics are radically different, and not just because Cai helped lead the revolution that toppled the former government. Ja-Long's family was powerful in the former government and so, of course, lost everything when the current government took power. Both are trained as soldiers, but they are more like figureheads."

"Too bad both sides won't agree to a prisoner exchange," Natalie said.

"That's what we've been trying to bring about," Denise said, "but neither side will budge. We're trying hard to defuse the situation, which is difficult to do with both men imprisoned."

One of the executives said, "We're hoping to get them to agree to a prisoner exchange. Both sides want their man out alive."

George glanced again at Cindy. Her brow was furrowed, she was holding very still, and she seemed very pale. Now George was certain Cindy had an idea. He tried to guess what it could be, but he was stumped. He hoped whatever she wanted to do did not involve any more hacking.

"We really think it would help if the six of you would make public statements to help our cause. You'll do that, right?"

"Of course we will," George said.

Cindy swallowed and summoned her courage to ask a question. "But how will our statements help bring about a prisoner exchange?"

"As you can see from your newspaper right there," Denise said, "the situation isn't being given headlines right now. The truth is that most people in the west don't care very much what is going on in that part of Asia. We're hoping that you'll be able to bring the public's attention to the situation."

Spider gestured toward the newspaper. "*We're* on the front page. People are interested in *us*."

"People are *very* interested in you," another of the executives said.

"It's easy to see why the president aimed his missile, isn't it?" Spider asked. "It got everyone's attention."

"Unfortunately, people are not paying attention

anymore," Denise said.

"I'm still not sure I understand your plan for getting both sides to exchange prisoners," Cindy said.

"I am afraid we don't have much of a plan," Denise said. "We're using the only tool we have. Diplomacy."

Cindy tried to contain her surprise. *Diplomacy?* That was *it?* Denise Williams was depending on diplomacy to bring about an exchange of prisoners—and whatever publicity the Knights of the Square Table might bring them? It was always a fresh surprise to Cindy to realize that adults, even adults who seemed as intelligent and competent as Denise Williams, in fact had no idea at all what they were doing.

"We're hoping that when you get back from California," Denise said, "you'll be able to help us draw world attention to the issue. You'll be back in two days."

"Oh, did we tell you?" George said. "Only four of us will be going to San Francisco."

"Really?" Denise asked. "Why?" She sounded faintly alarmed.

"We just decided that would be best," George said. "Cindy and I would like to return to the island or wait in Iceland for the others to come back." Denise was still frowning, so George said, "Veronica Hollick is still there. I'm sure Don will take us."

"Won't you need to be here to mount your public relations campaign?" one of the directors asked.

"My parents are returning with us," Liam said,

"to install a communication system on the island. All we need is access to the Internet and we'll be all set, right?"

"Right," said Denise. "And a good camera for recording videos, which we'll give you."

After that, there was silence. George was pretty sure the meeting was over. So he said, politely, "Would you mind if we have some time to ourselves?"

"Of course not," Denise said. "Feel free to stay here in the room. Your cabs will be here in about a half hour."

23

The moment the six of them were alone, George turned to Cindy and said, "Okay. Tell us."

Cindy looked at him, amazed. "How do you know?"

"I just know," George said.

"*What* do you know?" Spider asked, feeling confused.

"Cindy has an idea," George said.

"Uh-oh!" Spider said, slapping his knee. "That means trouble! Where are we hacking next, Cindy?"

"We're not hacking anymore," Alexis said, putting her hands on her hips. "We promised. Remember?"

"Exactly," Cindy said. "No more hacking."

"Okay," George said to Cindy. "Then tell us your idea."

"Here's what I think," Cindy said. "Right now, both sides are at a stalemate. Neither can move without going into check. Denise thinks she can bring about a prisoner exchange through diplomacy, even though she has no negotiating power at all.

What are the chances of that working, even if George makes the most amazing speech possible?"

"About zero," Liam said. "But what can we do?"

"Unless there's a miracle," Cindy said, "there won't be a prisoner exchange, and the worst thing would be for both sides to execute their prisoners. So we prevent the prisoners from being executed by offering to bring both Cai and Ja-Long to our island." Cindy crossed her arms over her chest and waited for the objections.

"You are crazy," Alexis told Cindy. "Flat-out mad. These are *soldiers*. They are *killers*. One of them led a *revolution*. They are dangerous men, and they are enemies."

"They're university graduates," Cindy said.

"And what does that have to do with anything?" Alexis demanded.

"I'm just saying that they've both been to the university in Beijing so they've been exposed to other ideas," Cindy said.

"So you don't think a university graduate can be dangerous?" Alexis demanded. "Do you really think all the bad guys dropped out of school?"

"That's not what I'm saying. I'm saying before all the fighting started, they were ordinary guys—or sort of ordinary. The articles I saw said there were always signs they could be leaders. But there's no sign that either of them is psychopathic or anything. They just firmly believe they're right. Maybe they're a little fanatical, but hey. Ja-Long just lost everything his family owns in a revolution. Cai is part of that revolution."

"Exactly," Alexis said. "They are sworn enemies. They've spent the past few months trying to *kill* each other."

"Besides," Spider said. "What will we do with them on the island?" He grinned. "Put them to work harvesting potatoes?"

"We will defuse the situation," Cindy said. "Neither can be executed if they're on the island. We save *both* of them from execution, which both sides will appreciate. Neither of them can cause any trouble on the island."

"Um, Cindy," Liam said. "Actually they can cause trouble on the island."

"Okay, but they can't cause trouble in *Asia*," Cindy said.

"There is only one small problem," Alexis said. "Nobody is going to let us do that. Our parents will have fits. Even the Nations United for Peace will not allow it. They'll say we are putting ourselves in danger. And they'll be *right*."

"That's why we don't ask permission ahead of time," Cindy said. "We announce our idea to the world and take everyone by surprise. There will be a lot of discussion and everyone will realize we're right."

"Do you think they'll *want* to come?" Spider asked.

"Which would you rather," Cindy asked him. "Get executed? Or go live on an island with a bunch of kids?"

"How will we bring them there?" Liam asked.

"In a helicopter," Cindy said.

"Don will put his foot down," Alexis said. "He's an easygoing sort of guy. But I can tell you he will not want to fly dangerous prisoners around in his helicopter."

"Don won't have to do it," Cindy said. "Look. We'll make an offer. Hopefully both sides will agree. If they agree, we'll have to get help bringing them back to the island."

Cindy looked around at the others. Liam had his arms crossed over his chest. Alexis was frowning. Spider was listening, alert. George seemed amused. Natalie was sitting back in her seat. Natalie was the one Cindy couldn't read.

Suddenly George burst out laughing. His laughter was so sudden and so surprising that they all turned to him as if he'd suddenly taken leave of his senses.

"What's so funny?" Cindy asked.

George recovered from his laughing fit and said, "Cindy, you are just so full of surprises." He looked at the others and said, "I saw Cindy at school all the time. Trust me, nobody at Lowell has any idea that Cindy is so unpredictable and, well, *subversive*. Everyone thinks she's shy and timid."

Meanwhile, Natalie hadn't moved. She was still sitting back in her seat, perfectly calm, her expression unreadable.

"Natalie?" Cindy asked. "What do you think?"

Natalie stood up and walked to the window. She had that intent look she got when she was thinking hard.

She stood perfectly still for a very long time. Then, she turned slowly to face the others. Speaking very softly she said, "I think it's a good idea."

"You *do*?" Liam asked.

"Yes," Natalie said.

"Aren't you afraid to have guys like that on our island?" Alexis asked.

"A little bit, yes," Natalie said, "but if the idea is to bring peace to the region, the idea is a good one. Get two of the leaders, including a guy likely to make trouble, out of the way."

"Yeah," Spider said, "by sending them to us. One side just has to raid our island, rescue their guy, capture the other guy, and there we are, in the middle of a war."

"I really don't think the Democratic Republic will attack us," George said. "Come on. I'm a local hero! Remember? They *love* me. I'm the guy who called on the whole world to send them all that aid and food. If they agree to the plan, I'm sure they won't raid us."

"What about the other side?" Spider said. "The refugees? The ones raising an army?"

"They can't raid our island," Natalie told Spider.

"Why not?" Spider asked.

Natalie smiled. "Because our island is in the middle of the North Atlantic. The refugees are *homeless*. Homeless people don't have helicopters."

Spider pointed to Natalie and said, "Good point."

"All right," Alexis said, "and then what? Do we keep them on our island *forever*?"

"No," Natalie said. "Just until the fighting stops. Bringing them to the island is just the first step. Like when we got that missile lowered. All anyone had to do was fix what we did and raise the missile again. But lowering the missile got rid of the emergency situation and gave us a chance to figure out what to do next. Offering to bring both prisoners to our island does the same thing. It takes away the immediate danger of executions and gives everyone a chance to figure out how to solve the refugee situation and diffuse all the anger."

"I still think it crazy," Alexis said.

"Maybe it is," Cindy said quietly. "Maybe *I'm* crazy."

"I don't know about crazy," Spider told her. "But you certainly are a girl with surprising ideas."

"Hey! Hacking into the bank was *your* idea," Cindy told him.

"Yeah," Spider said, "but *actually doing* it was yours."

"I'll tell you why I like Cindy's idea," George said. "Denise Williams and the other leaders of Nations United for Peace want us because we're celebrities. They want us because they want their peace-making efforts to be on the front pages instead of the fifth page. But Cindy's idea lets us really solve the problem, not just smile for the cameras and get the story on the front pages."

Natalie realized Liam hadn't said anything at all. "Liam?" she asked. "What do you think?"

It took him several moments to answer. At last,

he said, "It's a very bold idea."

The others took his statement to be one of agreement. She knew better, though. She knew he was doubtful. In fact, she understood exactly what Liam had done. By stating a fact, he'd been able to avoid giving his opinion. He had reservations, but he wasn't prepared to derail the idea.

"So we're all agreed?" George asked. "Anyone object to the idea?"

Nobody objected.

"Okay," George said, "if we're going to do this, I think I should call the president of the Democratic Republic once more."

"What are you going to tell him?" Alexis asked.

"I'm going to tell him that I have a plan for saving his nephew's life. It's important to get maximum credit for everything we do. I think of it as building good will."

"But don't tell *anyone* the details ahead of time," Alexis said. "*Especially* our parents."

24

Most of the passengers had already boarded Flight 109 direct to San Francisco when Spider, Natalie, Liam, and Alexis entered the plane.

Spider was the first to step into the cabin. The moment he entered the plane, with Alexis directly behind him, the passengers aboard burst into clapping and cheers. People whipped out cell phones and snapped their pictures. As Spider and the others walked down the aisle toward their seats, passengers gave them high fives and thumbs-up.

"I guess none of the haters are on this plane," Alexis whispered to Spider.

Their seats were in the very last row. Spider stood back and let Natalie sit by the window. Alexis sat next to Natalie. Spider preferred to sit in the aisle. He was unable to sit still for long, and being on the aisle allowed him to jump up and stretch his legs when he felt he had to.

Liam sat across the aisle next to a stranger. He said hello to the woman next to him—he felt he should be friendly. The woman, it turned out, spoke very little English, so Liam didn't have to worry about making polite conversation. He told her he liked music and put on his earphones.

After the pilot's announcement about flight times and weather conditions, one of the flight attendants said, "Ladies and gentlemen, we ask everyone to give the youngsters in the back their privacy so they can enjoy their flight home to visit their families."

At that, the entire plane burst again into applause.

Once they were in the air, the flight attendants came to tell them that their tickets included complimentary use of the Internet, so they were free to turn on their electronic devices.

Spider opened his email and started reading. He grinned and leaned forward so he could talk to all the others at once. "Looks like we're all going to my grandfather's restaurant after we get home."

"I see that!" said Alexis, who had just read an email from her mother.

Spider's grandfather's restaurant typically closed between two and five during the week. Their plane was scheduled to arrive just before two. Spider's grandfather invited all the families for a private late afternoon get-together complete with fresh pasta and pizza.

"And we're going in my dad's cab," Natalie said, reading her email. Her father would be waiting at the airport to take them directly to the restaurant. Initially her uncle was going to come with two cabs, thinking six of them were arriving, but with only four and not much baggage they could all squeeze into one cab.

Alexis was reading the news when she said, "Hey, look at this!" She passed around her phone so they could each see the article. Someone asked the president of the Democratic Republic to comment on the statement George had made when asked about the timing of the phone calls. The president had said, "George Cheung is an honorable young man."

Natalie received a message from Liam. "I know you like the idea," he wrote. "I'm just not sure. It might be kind of crazy."

She looked out the window. What she liked about flying over the clouds was the shocking blue of the sky. It occurred to her that flying in an airplane was such an impossible, preposterous thing to be able to do—zooming through the sky, high above the clouds, traveling over half the globe in only nine hours. If you went back in time a few thousand years and told people that one day it would be possible for people to fly around the world in jets, they would have never believed it.

"Maybe it is a little crazy," Natalie emailed back. "Or maybe Cindy's a visionary."

"I guess it's hard to tell the difference," he responded.

* * *

As they approached San Francisco, a flight attendant came to speak to them. "Security officers will escort you to your cab," she said. "We've been told there is a mob of reporters waiting for you."

Natalie, sitting on the aisle, thanked her. When the flight attendant left, Natalie said, "What will we do without George?"

"We just won't answer questions," Spider said. "I sure can't do what he does."

The landing was a smooth one. Because they were seated in the back of the plane, they were the last to exit. Even though Natalie was expecting the security officers, being greeted at the gate by people wearing uniforms gave her something of a shock. It wasn't long ago, after all, she would have expected uniformed officers to escort her to a federal prison.

The officers had one of those electric-powered carts they used for people who needed rides to their gates. All four piled in with their backpacks and bags. Natalie had never ridden in one of these carts before, but she saw right away why riding through the airport on a cart was a good idea. There was a group of reporters waiting for them just on the other side of the security checkpoint, but they were able to zoom right past them.

They didn't need to go to baggage claim. None of them had checked any baggage through, so the officers drove them directly to the door leading to the street.

Natalie's father was waiting just outside in his cab. Seeing them, he sprang from the driver's seat and gave Natalie a tight hug. The other three slid into the back seat. Natalie got into the passenger's seat, and her father walked back around to his door, sat in the driver's seat, and shifted gears.

He swung into traffic and turned onto Highway 101 toward San Francisco. "So where are the other two?" he demanded.

"George and Cindy didn't come," Natalie said.

"Why the heck not?"

Natalie hesitated. "I think I'd better let them do their own explaining." To change the subject, she looked out the window and said, "It feels like I've been gone forever."

"Girl," her father said, "look at my head!" He whipped off his hat. "Do you see all those gray hairs? Do you see how many more I've gotten in the last three months? Do you know what a fright you gave us?"

"I know, Dad. I'm sorry." She smiled. "But come on. It was probably days before you even realized I was gone!"

He looked at the others in the rearview mirror. "There's a lot of commotion at our house."

"You can say that again," Natalie said.

Natalie's father sighed heavily. "Natalie. The good girl. The one who never gave us a moment of trouble." He looked back at the others and said, "She was even a quiet baby. She hardly ever cried."

"That's because there would have been no point," Natalie said. "Who would have even heard?"

"Very funny," he said. "Our house isn't *that* noisy." He looked back into the rearview mirror and said, "Then one day we find a letter asking us not to call the police because our little Natalie might get in big trouble. Next we see her face on all the news programs." He sighed again. "And now I am very gray."

"You look *great*, Dad," Natalie said.

"You're going back to that island again?" he asked. "Are you nuts?"

"Cindy worries that we might be," Natalie said. "We just got back from Switzerland."

"Yeah, I know all about that," he said. "You're going to solve all the problems in the world, right?"

"Well, maybe not *all* of them," Alexis said.

Natalie's father raised his eyebrows and glanced at Alexis in the rearview mirror. "You're a smart one, too, right? Natalie was always the smart one in our house. Got all A's without even trying. All those test scores they send home from school? Natalie's scores were as high as you get. Too smart for her own britches, my mother used to say. Watch that girl, she said. A girl that smart is going to get herself into trouble. But I always thought *nah*, not Natalie. Sweet little Natalie won't ever get into trouble." He sighed again. "Now here we are."

Natalie's father took the Fourth Street exit, and merged onto Bryant Street. Natalie always found it unnerving the way her father drove. He fulfilled all the stereotypes of a typical cab driver: He careened around corners, zoomed in and out of lanes, and honked at startled pedestrians. But he always got where he was going very quickly. He liked to joke about the time the speedometer in his cab was not working properly and he got everywhere in half the expected time.

Having two cab drivers in the family came in handy. Each morning, Natalie went to school in a taxi. When she was younger, her classmates thought she was rich. When she was in kindergarten, a fifth-grade girl had said, "Wow! You come to school in a *taxi*?" Getting out of a taxi in front of the school each morning made her feel like a princess.

"Marissa wants to go with you when you leave again," Natalie's father said.

"I know," Natalie said. She looked at her father to see how he felt about this, but she couldn't tell because he was too intent on the traffic. "Well," Natalie said, "it's not like an island near Iceland is *that* far away."

"Yeah, right," her father said, "I guess we should be glad you didn't decide to go to another *planet*."

He took the direct route to North Beach, which meant driving through Union Square and the most congested traffic in the city at this time of day. But traffic didn't faze her father. He seemed to believe that honking could clear up a traffic jam. He merged left onto Columbus Avenue, the main thoroughfare through North Beach. They were at a stoplight when he turned to Natalie and said, "You've given your word, right? No more hacking? No more breaking the law?"

"No more hacking," Natalie said. "No more breaking the law."

"Do you promise?" he demanded. "I don't want to have to worry about you anymore."

"I promise." Then she repeated, "No more hacking. No more breaking the law." She didn't look into the backseat. She imagined that the others were keeping their expressions carefully neutral.

Her father, of course, was asking the wrong questions.

25

"There are a lot of reporters at the restaurant," Spider said. "I just got a text from my dad."

"How do they know where we're going?" Alexis asked.

"They followed our mothers," Spider said. "Smart, right?"

The restaurant was on Union Street in North Beach, partway up the west-facing side of Telegraph Hill. Natalie's father pulled to a stop in front of the restaurant. He'd been planning to drop them off, and go find a place to park the cab. But they all stared, stunned, at what they saw.

In front of the restaurant was a huge mob of people, mostly men, holding cameras. "They're all waiting for us?" Natalie asked.

"It sure looks like it," Spider said.

"What do we do?" Natalie asked.

The door to the restaurant was locked with a "closed" sign in front. "Let me call my dad," Spider said. He took out his cell phone. When his father answered, he said, "We're outside in a cab! How are we going to get past all those guys?"

Spider listened for a moment, then said, "Okay!" and hung up. To the others, he said, "We're going to run for it. My dad is right inside and will open the door for us. Just before we go in, we can pose for pictures. My dad thinks that's all they want."

"Don't they want to interview us?"

"My dad gave them George's phone number and email address and said George does the talking for the group," Spider said. "Just like I asked him to."

Alexis slung her backpack over her shoulder. "Everyone ready?" she asked.

"I am," Natalie said.

"Let's go," Liam said.

They all opened their doors at once and ran to the restaurant door.

"Here are four of them!" one of the men shouted.

Once they reached the door, they all four turned to face the reporters. They smiled and waved while dozens of cameras flashed.

Some of the reporters were shouting questions: "How long will you be home? When are you returning to your island?"

"You'll have to talk to George about all that!" Spider called out.

Spider's father opened the restaurant door, and all four of them slipped inside. The moment they were in, Spider's father closed and locked the door.

The reporters were still shouting questions.

"Wow," Alexis said.

Natalie's entire family—her mother, her grandparents, her siblings—were in the restaurant. They'd pushed several tables together near a wall. The place, in fact, was packed. It was almost like walking into the airport after their rescue earlier that spring, except the space was tiny and everyone was subdued. From the ovens came the buttery smell of baking pizza crust.

"You guys may have missed having a washing machine," Spider said. "I missed pizza."

Liam's parents came to greet him. "Mom," Liam said. "Dad." He gave them each a hug.

Spider's grandfather put a large pizza on the table in front of them. Liam reached for a piece.

Alexis, her parents, and her sister found a quiet booth and sat together, talking. Liam stood awkwardly with his parents. He wanted to talk to them, but he wasn't sure what to say. They'd already talked several times on the phone and exchanged a half dozen emails. The others seemed so much more at ease with their parents.

"Thanks for putting in a communication system for us," Liam said.

"We couldn't get tickets on the same flight," his father said. "But we'll meet you at the airport in Iceland."

"Are you both going?" Liam asked them.

"Just me," said his father. "I'm bringing Roger Raine. He's the guy I told you about who will know how to tie in to the satellite system." His father smiled and said, "We'll have a lot of metal in our baggage," he said. "We may have some explaining to do at the airport."

A knock came at the door. Spider's grandfather went to see who it was. Everyone inside grew quiet. "A couple with a teenage boy," Spider's grandfather said. "Does anyone know who they are?"

Alexis ran to the glass and looked out. "Cindy's parents and her brother!" she said.

Spider's grandfather opened the door and let them in. You could see right away from the expressions on Cindy's parents' faces that they were distressed and confused.

"She didn't come back," Cindy's mother said.

Natalie went to greet them. "Cindy was afraid you wouldn't let her leave again," Natalie said gently. "And we have important work to do."

Natalie could see that this entirely failed to comfort Cindy's parents. "What has gotten into her?" her mother asked. "She was never like this before."

Natalie wasn't sure how to answer this.

"She needs to quit this group," her father said. "I don't want her mixed up in any of this."

Surprised, Natalie looked around. Alexis was standing by, listening. She saw Liam edge closer so he, too, could listen. Alexis put her hands on her hips the way she did when she was gearing up for an argument. The last thing Natalie wanted, though, was for Alexis to start arguing with Cindy's parents. Alexis was a bit of a powerhouse.

Natalie gestured to Alexis to stay back. Quietly to Alexis, Natalie said, "I'll talk to them." Then, she turned to Cindy's parents and said, very gently, "Cindy thinks she can bring about peace on earth."

"Who does she think she is?" Cindy's father demanded. "Joan of Arc?"

"No, of course not," Natalie said, feeling confused. "Wasn't Joan of Arc a warrior?"

"Joan of Arc believed she heard voices telling her she had to perform great deeds," Cindy's father said.

"Oh, no, I'm sure Cindy doesn't hear voices," Natalie said. "She just really thinks we can create peace on earth. How can that be a bad thing?"

Suddenly lots of people started talking at once. Someone said, "It's absurd!" Someone else said, "We shouldn't be allowing this." In the hubbub that followed, Natalie walked over to Alexis and whispered, "If we can't get our parents behind us, how are we going to get the whole world behind us?"

"Good point," Alexis whispered back. "The question is, without George here, how are we going to get *anyone* behind us?"

Just then, though, another knock came at the door. At the same time, Alexis's phone rang. She answered it, listened, and then said aloud, "Tammy is outside!"

"Who is Tammy?" Liam's father asked.

"Veronica's aunt," Liam told him.

"Can we let her in?" Alexis asked.

Spider's grandfather opened the door just wide enough for Tammy to enter, pulling two large suitcases behind her. She dropped her suitcases just inside the door, and reached over to give Alexis a quick hug.

"If I would have known every reporter in town was going to be taking my picture," Tammy said, "I would have dressed a little nicer!"

"You look great," Alexis told her.

"I feel great." She pulled an airline ticket out of her handbag and said, "I'm going with you!"

Natalie's mother, sitting on a stool at the counter not far away, said, "*You're* going back with them?"

"You bet I am," Tammy said. "If they'll let me. These kids have their own *island*! How cool is that? It's too bad it's not located a little closer to the equator, but you can't have everything, right?"

"Good," Natalie's mother said. "You can keep an eye on them."

To Natalie, Alexis whispered, "Nobody needs to keep an eye on us."

Natalie changed her mind about the best way to proceed. "Maybe you'd better take over," Natalie told Alexis. "I think you need to make a speech."

"Okay," Alexis said. "I may not have as much finesse as George, but I can do it." She cleared her throat loudly, and clapped for attention. "All right, everyone," Alexis said loudly. "Listen up!"

The room quieted.

"I don't have George's gift for making speeches," Alexis said, "but I have something important to say." She paused and looked around. "Here it is. You're gonna all have to trust us, okay? We don't need looking after. We stopped a *war*, for gosh sakes. We promised not to do any more hacking, and we won't. But you have to just let us do things our way for a little while, all right?"

Liam glanced at his parents to see how they were responding to being given instructions by a fifteen-year-old. Both of them were staring at Alexis, amazed.

Natalie's father said, "Fine. But I'm glad you're letting adults go with you."

"Anyone can come with us," Alexis said. "But it's *our* island, so *our* rules."

"What *are* the rules?" Tammy asked.

"You tell them, Natalie," Alexis said.

Natalie smiled. "We basically only have one. Be nice."

Marissa clapped and said, "Go, girls!" Cindy's brother Mark clapped, stamped his feet, and whistled. Eventually a few others clapped as well. Most, like Cindy's and Liam's parents, sat quietly.

26

Alexis and her family were the first to leave. Tammy went with them. There was an empty apartment in the building where Tammy could spend the night. Alexis stood at the door with her parents, her sister, and Tammy, saying good-bye to everyone and then, "See you all tomorrow at the airport!"

It was almost five o'clock and Spider's grandfather was getting ready to open the restaurant for the dinner rush. "You're all welcome to stay," he assured the families that remained.

That was when Liam realized that Spider had fallen asleep with his head on a table. Liam pointed to Spider. Spider's father grinned and said, "The jet lag will hit you all pretty soon."

It was late afternoon in California, but for those who had woken up early that morning on an island not far from Iceland, it felt like 1:00 a.m.

Spider's father tapped Spider on the shoulder and woke him up. "Why don't you go to bed?"

"Good idea," Spider said, yawning again. He told everyone good night, and shuffled off through the kitchen, his head drooping. His father went with him, probably to make sure he made it all the way to a bed without falling asleep on the way.

That left Liam and Natalie.

And Liam had an idea.

∗ ∗ ∗

Natalie's uncle was on his way with another cab, and her family was getting ready to leave. Liam maneuvered himself until he was standing next to Natalie and said, "I am not looking forward to getting my picture taken out there."

"Me, neither!" she said.

"I'll bet if we sneak out the back, no one will recognize us. I saw an alley back there. We can go through the alley, and go home on Muni in peace and quiet. Put your hair in this hat and nobody will know it's you." He handed her the cobalt blue knit hat he often wore.

"*Great* idea." She turned to her parents and said, "Can I?"

"I was worrying how we were going to get everyone home with only two cabs," her mom said.

"Do you want me to go with you?" Marissa asked Natalie. "A famous girl shouldn't be riding Muni alone."

"I can take her all the way home," Liam said.

Liam saw from Marissa's suddenly alert expression and the way she raised her eyebrows that she understood exactly what Liam was up to.

"You have your phone with you, right?" Natalie's

mother asked.

"Yes!" Natalie said. She turned to Marissa. "Can you take my backpack for me?"

"No problem." Marissa picked up the backpack and slung it over her shoulder. "This is heavy!"

"Packed with dirty clothes!" Natalie said.

"I'll throw them in the wash for you," Marissa said.

"Thanks!" Natalie said.

Meanwhile, Liam went to tell his parents what he was doing. "All right," his father said. "See you later."

Liam and Natalie said their good-byes, and went through the kitchen and into the small yard in back. The pavement was cracked with weeds coming up. A few lawn chairs were in a corner. The fence was badly in need of repair. Just across the yard was a gate leading to the alley.

They slipped through the gate. There were a few people walking briskly through the alley, but nobody paid any attention to them. "This way," Liam said. They walked uphill, which meant away from the bus lines, but it was the quickest way out of the alley.

They reached the street, then turned right and walked to the corner. There, to the left, at the top of the hill, was Coit Tower, a slender, fluted concrete column. To the right, down the hill, was Columbus Street, the busy thoroughfare. About twenty feet down the sidewalk was also where the horde of reporters was waiting with their cameras. They were watching the restaurant.

Seeing the reporters, Liam and Natalie whirled around and walked back in the opposite direction, toward Filbert Street. "I think we should go up," Liam said, pointing toward the tower with his thumb. "We can go down the other side on Green Street."

"Okay," she said. If she understood his maneuvers, she was acting like she didn't. His aim was to go to Pioneer Park, the wooded area surrounding the tower. He'd never been there with a girl. You'd think that being on the island for so many months meant lots of opportunity to be alone, but in fact, you never knew when someone might come along, so you could never really feel alone. In some ways, life with a group on an island was like living in a goldfish bowl.

They passed the alley, and reached Filbert Street. They turned right and headed up toward the tower. The street was thronged with tourists taking pictures and locals walking their dogs.

"If we take pictures with our cell phones," Natalie whispered, "we'll look just like tourists!"

"George wouldn't be hiding from reporters," Liam whispered back. "He'd call this a publicity opportunity."

"Without George here, I'd call this an opportunity to say the wrong thing. I would have *fainted* if someone had asked me that question about the timing of the calls."

"Yeah," Liam said. "I would have started stammering and stuttering."

Pioneer Park was only four blocks up. The hitch

was that to get there, you had to walk up a hill so steep that the sidewalk was a set of stairs. Filbert Street was narrow, with cars parked parallel to the curb, leaving almost no room for driving.

Once they reached the top, they turned left onto the path that took them past the entrance to the tower to the lookout spot. From the treetops came the distinctive chirping and screeching of birds.

"The parrots," Liam said.

"Oh, yeah," Natalie said. She'd forgotten about the flock of parrots on Telegraph Hill.

They reached the lookout point, and jumped over the low west-facing wall. They walked down the hill a short distance, away from the tourists taking pictures on the summit. Below them was the Bay. To the right was the Bay Bridge, to the left, the Golden Gate Bridge. The fog was coming in from the ocean, swirls of clouds moving over the bridge towers.

You'd think the top of a hill would be quiet, but not Telegraph Hill in the late afternoon. They were close enough to the Embarcadero, a main roadway that ran along the wharfs, to hear the sound of cars and the honking of horns, and even an occasional boat horn. Add in what sounded like dozens of screeching parrots in the trees and you had a situation.

"Let's sit for a few minutes," he suggested.

"Okay," she said, sitting on a bench. "It is *noisy*."

Liam sat beside her. "It's a beautiful noise," he said. "A melody harmonized from strife."

She looked at him. "You're a poet, Liam."

He put his fingers to his lips. "Shh," he whispered. "Don't tell anyone."

"Why not?"

"Because nobody likes the nerdy guy who plays the saxophone and likes poetry."

"Someone does," she said quietly.

She looked so beautiful just then, with a few stray curls escaping from the knit cap. He liked seeing her wearing his hat. He felt he should look away, but he couldn't. Sitting this close to her set his pulse racing.

"We should be here at night," he said. "The city would be all lit up."

"We can *imagine* it's night," she said.

Liam took that as encouragement. He moved closer to her, and touched her chin. Then he kissed her.

* * *

They walked down the northwest-facing side of the hill, on a charming trail that took them past houses with terraced gardens and low stone walls, toward the Embarcadero. There, they could board the F-Market toward downtown, where they'd switch to a bus heading out to the Mission area, where Natalie lived.

At first, they walked holding hands, but after a while, the path was too narrow and too steep to walk side by side, and people in a hurry kept trying to pass them. So they walked single file with Natalie in front. About halfway down, she paused at a lookout spot. Just below was the Bay and Treasure Island. The water was the same steely gray as the sky. From where they stood, they could see rush-hour traffic backed up on the Bay Bridge. A flock of seagulls lifted into the air.

Quietly, Natalie said, "Not on the island, okay? I don't want anyone to know."

He swallowed. It was a moment before he could speak. "Because of Spider?"

"I don't want his feelings hurt. After a while it won't matter. I think Spider and Alexis will get together and he'll forget about me. Until then, I don't want anything to happen."

"Okay," he said. He didn't like it, but he understood. She wanted to be nice.

27

When Spider's father left him upstairs in his grandparents' apartment, he laid down on the bed in the guest room.

He was suddenly wide awake. He stared for a while at the ceiling, thinking about Cindy's latest idea. He hadn't been the slightest bit worried about hacking into a bank, mostly because nobody could get hurt. But he couldn't make up his mind how he felt about this idea of bringing two prisoners to their island. Was it foolish, or daring? He didn't know. It occurred to him that there was a fine line between bravery and stupidity.

Since he obviously wasn't sleeping, he thought about going back down to the restaurant, but he decided against it. Any minute now, the jet lag would hit him again. Instead, he thought he should close the windows. Darkness might help him sleep.

He was pulling the curtains closed when he saw Liam and Natalie walking together through the backyard to the alley. Natalie's hair was stuffed into Liam's blue knit cap. Watching, Spider's heart turned over in his chest. He turned and ran out of the room, up the stairs to the third floor. The east-facing window on the third floor had a view of both streets.

He saw them reach the corner of Union Street. They stood for just a moment, as if deciding what to do. Then they turned and headed back toward Filbert. He watched until they turned right at the corner.

They were going to Pioneer Park.

He went back to the bed, laid down, and closed his eyes. There were hidden trails in that park on the top of that hill, so many places to be alone—or, well, as alone as you could be in the middle of a major city in late afternoon. It was, in Spider's opinion, the perfect place to go with a girl.

He remembered his exact words that day last spring when he'd asked her to go with him: *Now that we're back*, he had said, *maybe we can do something together—just us? I know a great path up to Coit Tower.* She hadn't wanted to go. But now, here she was, going with Liam.

Ever since that morning when they were on their way to Canada and he saw Natalie and Liam emerge from the woods, he'd suspected this was happening. The difference was that before he had only suspected. Now he *knew*. He fell asleep feeling completely miserable.

* * *

Spider was the first to arrive at the departure gate the next day. No reporters were waiting for him. He sent

George a text: *"No reporters are here!"*

It was nice to be able to communicate again with electronics.

"That's because I told them you're leaving this evening," George wrote back.

"Ha ha. World leaders aren't supposed to lie," Spider wrote back.

"Lying to paparazzi doesn't count," George responded.

"Ha ha," Spider wrote again. *"See you in about ten hours."*

He put his phone back into his pocket. He overheard snippets of conversation around him. People were talking about the city, the weather, nothing of weight. You wouldn't know, to glance around, that there was a crisis brewing in Asia. In superhero movies, the enemy was always an evil villain out to destroy the world. In the real world, the enemy wasn't an evil villain. The real enemy was apathy.

"You're looking glum," came Alexis's voice behind him.

He turned. "Hi," he said. That was when he became aware of his posture. He'd been sitting slumped in the seat with his arms crossed over his chest, his backpack and extra carry-on at his feet.

Alexis walked around the set of chairs. She carried a full backpack and pulled a suitcase on wheels.

She sat down beside him. "What's the matter?"

He shrugged. He knew better than to say,

"Nothing," when something was bothering him. It would sound like a lie. Lying to paparazzi might be acceptable, but not to your best friends.

It occurred to him that she might get the wrong idea. She might think he was glum about leaving home and returning to Mars.

So he gave her a truthful answer. "I make too many jokes," he said. "I need to stop." What he was thinking was, *I need to be a little more serious. Like Liam.*

"Excuse me, *what?*" She turned, put one hand on her hip, and looked directly at him. "You're *hilarious!* Everyone likes your jokes."

"I need to get more serious," he said.

"Why? There's enough *serious* in the world."

Just then, he was glad Alexis had a propensity to argue with everything. The conversation was turning fun.

"The thought occurred to me that I should stop joking so much."

"Take that thought right out of your head," she said. "You're *great* just the way you are."

He looked closely at her. She meant what she said—he could see that. But then, one thing about Alexis was that she always meant what she said. He wondered if she ever experienced self-doubt. If she did, she sure didn't act like it. But she obviously knew how to give a pep talk when someone else was feeling miserable.

"Thanks," Spider said. What he felt was a rush of gratitude—and affection.

"Hey!" Alexis said. "There's Liam!" She waved to

Liam, who was coming toward them with a backpack and a small duffel bag.

"Hi, guys," he said.

That was when Spider noticed a woman sitting in a chair not far away, watching them. She stood up and came toward them, saying, "Excuse me, you're Spider, right? And Alexis, and Liam?"

"Hi!" Alexis said. "Yup, that's us."

"I just want to tell you how much I admire everything you've done," she said. She took out her phone and said, "Would you mind if I took a picture?"

Alexis shrugged and looked at Liam and Spider. "Why not?" she said.

"We can take a selfie!" the woman said. Spider and Alexis stood up. They all huddled together. The woman held up her camera and took the picture.

Suddenly, they were surrounded by people asking if they, too, could have pictures. Not knowing what else to do—and not wanting to be rude—they spent the next twenty minutes posing for pictures with the waiting passengers. When Natalie arrived, she, too, was pulled into the pictures.

At last, an airport official came over to see what the fuss was. Seizing the opportunity to get a break, Alexis said, "I think we've done enough pictures, okay, everyone?"

"I think so too," the airport official said. "This plane will soon be boarding."

28

George's younger brother called him for the third time that morning. Now that George's family realized they could call him anytime they wanted, they called often and were a little less angry that he hadn't come home.

George talked to his brother for a few minutes. When he hung up, he checked the website showing the progress of Flight 793 from San Francisco to Iceland, with a stop in Chicago. "They'll soon be over the Atlantic," George said.

Cindy, George, and Don were at a hotel on the grounds of the Keflavík International Airport. Cindy's room was across the hall. Don was sitting on the bed, leaning back against the headboard, reading a book. Cindy and George were using their phones to surf the web and send email.

The rooms were done in a minimalist style. Three of the walls were white. The third was painted pea green. There were two twin-size beds with metal frames, and a small table with a simple lamp between the beds. The desk was a board mounted to the wall.

There was only one chair in the room, a simple metal chair, so they had brought over the chair from Cindy's room. That way both Cindy and George could sit at the desk.

Both George and Cindy felt their phones vibrate at the same time. Denise Williams had sent an email to all six of them at once. She wrote to tell them what they knew from the news websites: Diplomacy was failing. Both sides were still refusing a prisoner exchange. Both sides were preparing to attack to get their own guy out of the other side's prison. With mounting tensions, it looked like both sides might execute their prisoners.

Denise therefore hoped they would begin their media publicity campaign right away.

"I'm getting a little tired of sitting in here," George said. "I'm ready for a walk."

"Me, too," Cindy said. "What do you want us to bring back for you?" she asked Don. "Are you hungry?"

"Bring back anything," he said. "Thanks." He took out his wallet and handed George some Icelandic money.

George picked up a pad of paper and a pen. He and Cindy left the room, closing the door quietly behind them. The building had an elevator—a *lift*, as the guy at the front desk called it—but they went down a back stairway. Outside the air was cool and damp, the skies overcast.

It took less than fifteen minutes to walk to the airport. In the main terminal, they found a cafeteria and bought hot dogs. There were plenty of tables and empty chairs, so they were able to find a place to sit in a quiet corner where they could talk without being overheard.

George took a bite of his hot dog, then said, "I think we should take everyone by surprise, including the folks at the Nations United for Peace."

"I agree," Cindy said.

Together, they drafted a post for their blog. They wrote the first draft on a sheet of paper, then typed it into an email message, which they sent to the others on the plane. It didn't take long before the others responded with comments and suggestions.

When they finished tinkering, the final draft looked like this:

Dear Jailors of Cai and Ja-Long:

This looks like a stalemate, doesn't it? Nobody can make a move without losing, so nobody can make a move.

Executing your prisoners would be a bad idea. At the same time, we understand that setting your prisoners free would be a bad idea. For that matter, trying to hold your prisoners there for a long time isn't the best idea either because you're inviting attack from the other side.

So you're stuck.

We'd like to help you out. In fact, we have a solution.

Both prisoners, Cai and Ja-Long, can come to our island and live with us in peace. We know Cai and Ja-Long won't mind. Mars isn't so bad. It's definitely better than being dead or in jail.

If you agree, we'll figure out how to send helicopters to bring the prisoners to our island. Both will be safe, and neither of them will be able to cause any trouble. In fact, we think they'll both <u>like</u> being on the island. We do.

Sincerely,
The Knights of the Square Table

* * *

Cindy and George both knew they should go back to the room. Neither, though, wanted to move.

"Your family isn't calling you all the time," George said, "like mine."

"My brother called a few times. My parents are too angry."

"They want you to go home?"

"They want me to go back to the way I was before. Spending all my time at home reading books. Spending all my time out of the house playing chess. Bringing home straight-A report cards."

"They like you as a timid little mouse," George said.

"Exactly. My mother is the one who gave me Rousseau's *The Social Contract.* She said, 'Cindy, I think you'll understand and appreciate what a great book this is. Most kids your age wouldn't be able to.' She said it helped change the world for the better. But it wasn't the book that changed the world—it was the people who made the changes happen. I guess my mother just wants me to read inspiring books. She just doesn't want me inspired to act."

"I have one favor to ask you," George said. She looked at him and waited. He said, "Don't go back to the way you were before."

She smiled. She didn't bother saying that she didn't think it was possible. It wasn't like you could say, *I think I'll just be a different kind of person,* or *I think I'll just go back to the way I was last year.*

George looked around the cafeteria. She had the feeling there was something more he wanted to say. She waited.

"Have you noticed," he said at last, "Spider and Alexis seem to be getting together."

"I did notice that."

She saw that he suddenly seemed nervous. She didn't remember ever seeing him uneasy in a conversation.

"And you know what else I think?" George said. "I think Liam and Natalie like each other, too."

"I think so, too," she said.

She wanted to know how he felt about these developments. She'd always figured all the guys would want Natalie. But he was watching her, obviously trying to see how she felt about all the pairing off.

"Does it bother you?" she asked him.

"No," he said, startled, "why would it bother me? It makes sense, actually. Liam and Natalie like poetry. Alexis and Spider like hiking."

That was when it occurred to her, for the first time, that George might like *her*. No sooner did the thought occur to her when a voice in her head said, *No way.* George would never go for her. She figured a guy who radiated such ease would want someone equally self-assured.

He leaned back in his chair and looked at her, his uneasiness gone. He said, "It's almost like Cupid has been flying around our island."

* * *

It was early evening and they were all at the heliport: the six Knights of the Square Table, Tammy, Don, Marissa, Liam's father, Roger Raine, and the pilot who came with the helicopter provided by the Nations United for Peace.

Liam's father and Roger Raine loaded their boxes into the first helicopter: five large crates of equipment for setting up a communication system, a box of heavy plastic tarps, and boxes of food. They'd packed the kind of compact food that was easy to carry and would last a long time: boxes of nutrition bars, crates of flat noodles, protein powder, freeze-dried meals. They also brought air mattresses and a manual pump to inflate them.

You could see right away the family resemblance between Liam and his father. Both had strong jawlines and heavy brows. But whereas Liam smiled often, his father was more serious. Roger appeared to be in his mid-thirties. He was tall and thin and wore a San Francisco Giants shirt.

Both helicopters started up their engines. George was the last to board. When it was his turn to step into the helicopter, he pulled out his phone. "Just a minute!" he shouted, to be heard over the engines.

He clicked a few buttons and posted their letter to the blog. That done, he climbed into the waiting helicopter. Spider helped him close the door and pull the heavy latch into place.

He and his buddies had decided to post the letter to their blog at the last possible moment. They wanted to be on the island and out of touch when the news went live so the public reaction could take its course before they weighed in. Besides, sometimes after having reporters talk to you everywhere you went, it was nice to just be on an island far away from publicity and paparazzi.

29

"Beautiful!" Tammy said as they were landing. The sun was so hidden by clouds that the light seemed purple, casting the hills in surreal shades of blue and white. In places, the sun broke through, lighting the hills. The island was calm and lovely.

After they landed, George took the newcomers for a tour while Alexis, Spider, and Liam unloaded the stuff from the helicopter.

"What's in this?" Alexis asked, trying to lift a metal chest closed with heavyweight metal fasteners secured with heavy-duty tape. "Cinderblocks?"

"Tools," Spider said. "I have an idea."

Spider had checked the toolbox into the plane with the baggage, so the first time the others saw it was after they'd landed in Iceland.

"What's your idea?" she asked.

"Come on, I'll show you." Spider jumped down from the helicopter, picked up the toolbox by the handle, and marched off toward the plane. Alexis and Liam followed.

They stopped when they got to the opening of

the cargo hold. Don's voice came from inside the plane.

"I don't *know* how they got to Canada," Don said. "They called me from Canada and said they were in trouble. I didn't think I could refuse."

Whoever he was talking to said something, but they couldn't hear what.

"I think he's talking to my dad," Liam whispered.

"*Of course* it occurred to me that I was doing something wrong," Don said. "Would you have rather had them picked up by law enforcement? Publicly humiliated?"

"You could have called one of us." The speaker's voice was faint, but Liam could hear it distinctly enough to know it was indeed his father.

"I could have," Don said. "You're right. But they're not babies or small children. I decided to trust them. I spent a week with them on this island, and I believed them trustworthy." After a long pause, he said, "You know what I think? I think these kids *are* capable of doing things adults can't do."

There was a sound from inside, like footsteps.

"I think they're coming," Spider whispered.

"Let's just go in," Liam whispered. "Don't let on that we heard."

Alexis went first. She climbed into the cargo hold, stepped on a crate, and pulled herself into the main part of the plane. Once she was inside, she reached back for the toolbox and Spider handed it to her.

Don came down the aisle and said, "What do you have there?"

"A toolbox," she told him. "Spider has an idea."

By then Spider and Liam had both pulled themselves up into the plane.

"Hi, Dad," Liam said.

"All right," Don said. "Let's hear this idea."

Liam's father stood back listening. Liam wasn't sure what, if anything, to say to his father. But then, he never really knew what to say to him.

"The seats in here are attached to those rails," Spider said, pointing to the steel rails that ran lengthwise along the floor. "I think we can unscrew the seats and move them around."

"You're right," Don said. "We can. If we have the right tools."

Spider pulled off the tape and opened the box so Don could peer inside.

"I also think we can take the seats apart," Spider said, "and figure out how to lay the back down flat to make a cot."

"Let's try," Don said.

All of them got busy with screwdrivers and wrenches. Getting the seats off the rails so they could be moved turned out to be easy. All they had to do was unscrew a few bolts. To create extra room, they laid a few dozen on their sides and stacked them out of the way. The harder part was opening up the seats and unscrewing the backs so that the seat backs could be laid flat like a cot. Once they figured out which bolts to loosen, they turned twenty of the chairs into cots.

"We can hang up some tarps if anyone wants a

private room," Spider said. "Or people can just sleep dormitory style."

"I like the idea of hanging up tarps," Don said.

So Veronica, Tammy, Roger, Liam's father, and Don each got a private room with tarps for walls and a seat laid flat for a bed.

* * *

After breakfast the next morning, they went in shifts to the hot tub, first the girls, then the guys. With all these new people on the island, they designated a time for the guys to bathe, and a time for the girls.

Spider was sorry their bathing routine had to change, but with so many adults on the island, it just wouldn't do to have the girls prancing around in their underwear. They redesigned the tarp dressing room, using rope to tie the tarp to large boulders, extending the walls over the water so that you could get into the water directly from the dressing room.

Spider spent the morning with Liam's father and Roger, working on the communication system. George and Cindy went to the beach to gather mussels for lunch. The others—except Veronica— were up on the hill, building. Veronica, suddenly shy with so many people around, went off by herself.

While Spider wasn't particularly interested in coding or electronics, he was very interested in machinery and anything mechanical. He was particularly interested in the box of machine parts Roger and Liam's father had brought. The largest box they brought contained a solar generator.

Tying into a satellite required setting up a small station, called a teleport, with hub equipment at one end, and an antenna with remote equipment on the other. The antenna, shaped like a dish, transmitted the signals to a machine that converted them and passed them to a router.

At last, Roger—who had been tinkering with the equipment—said, "I think we've got it. I'm getting a signal."

* * *

Meanwhile, up on the hill, Liam was spreading the mortar while Alexis pressed the stones into place. They were finishing the stone front of yet another of their sod houses. Soon they would have an actual village.

Just after they fit a particularly large stone into place, they heard a man's angry voice coming from the direction of the plane.

"Is someone *yelling*?" Alexis asked.

They all held still and listened.

"It sounds like my dad," Liam said. "And he sounds *really* mad."

Liam, Natalie, and Alexis grew still and looked at each other.

"I guess they got online," Alexis said.

"What is going on?" Tammy asked. She looked at Marissa and asked, "Do you know?"

"I have no clue," Marissa said.

The shouting was louder now. Liam's father was coming up the hill, shouting, "Liam! Where *are* you,

Liam?"

"I'd better go talk to him," Liam said. He took off running toward the trail that led down the hill. The others followed, but kept a distance behind.

Liam's father's face was red with fury. Ordinarily he was calm and unflappable, so seeing him this way was a shock to Liam.

"Dad?" Liam asked.

"No," his father said. "You are *not* bringing two dangerous men to this island."

Liam glanced back. The others had stopped a little distance away, but close enough to hear everything. Liam felt intensely self-conscious. He turned to his father. "Dad, we should sit down and talk."

"I said no, Liam," he said. "The answer is *no*."

Liam searched for a way to tell his father that nobody was asking his permission, but couldn't think of how to do it. So he asked, "What was the public reaction? Did you see the news reports?"

"Of course I saw the news reports. That was the first thing I saw once we tied into the satellite. The answer is no. We let you come back here. We didn't stop you. It made sense to let you be public figureheads for that organization for a while. But you may *not* do this."

Liam sensed that the best way to proceed was to pretend that his father was, in fact, in charge. As Alexis had said at the restaurant, if they couldn't get their parents behind them, how would they get the whole world behind them?

"Why can't we?" Liam asked.

"Because the idea is insane. These men are dangerous."

That was when Liam realized his father was frightened, not angry.

"Do you really think they'll hurt us?" Liam asked. "We're saving them from execution. We're diffusing a dangerous situation. That part of Asia is on the brink of war again. Think how awful a war would be, Dad. Thousands of people would die. Or more. Wouldn't it be a good thing if we can prevent that?"

"Son, do you *honestly* think you can stop a war?"

Liam folded his arms across his chest. "Dad. We *did* stop a war. A *nuclear* war. Remember?"

"I'll tell you what," his father said. "I think there's more to that story than any of you are telling. I don't believe you called this dictator, said some magic words, and he suddenly decided he wanted peace. Personally, I think you kids did something else illegal, or you got very lucky."

Liam blinked, startled to realize his father was partly right. In addition to blackmail being unethical at best, they did have some good luck. They had succeeded *mostly* on their ingenuity and skills— George's ability to talk anyone into anything, Alexis's coding skills, Cindy's amazing memory, and Natalie's idea to gently blackmail the president. But they'd also gotten lucky with that bug in the Javelin program. Then they'd gotten lucky with the bank reacting to the publicity by donating even more money and asking that the hackers not be prosecuted.

In fact, maybe knowing they'd gotten lucky was part of why Liam himself was doubtful that they'd actually be able to accomplish anything other than act as celebrity figureheads and help with publicity.

But here was his father, ordering him around as if he was a child of five, instead of a young man who had achieved international celebrity because he and his friends had done a few amazing things.

"You underestimate us, Dad," Liam said quietly. "We *did* stop a nuclear war."

"I'm afraid you're playing dangerous games, son."

"I need to stick with my friends," Liam said quietly enough so the others wouldn't hear. "Besides, just what if it works? What if we can bring peace to the region? Wouldn't that be pretty incredible?"

"I just don't know about any of this." Liam's father no longer sounded angry. Now he seemed weary.

"I agree with what Alexis said at the restaurant," Liam said. "We have to do things our way for a little while."

His father considered this. "All right. Fine. We'll do things your way for a little while. But I'm staying right here on this island."

* * *

When they arrived back at the plane, Roger and Spider were inside, sitting in the first row with a laptop open on a crate in front of them. On the screen was a news website. Cindy and George, who had been at the beach gathering mussels, were also in the plane, looking at their phones.

"You kids did it again," Roger said. "You got the whole world's attention."

"The response is mixed," Cindy said. "We expected that, though, right? Some people are shocked. Some are intrigued. Some people think it's a brilliant idea. Some people think it's crazy. Jacy Skye tweeted about us again."

"Really?" Liam asked. "What did she tweet?"

"She's calling us the Wonder Kids. It looks like both sides are going to agree to let us have their prisoners."

They all sat down and turned on their phones. To get Internet access, each needed to punch in the access code that Roger had written down for them. "For now you can only get Internet access in the plane, or very close by," Roger told them as he handed them the access code.

Once they were online, they found that each of them had received an email from Denise Williams. "We knew that having the six of you on the team would help focus the world's attention on our issues," she wrote. "But we never expected you to come up with something so startling."

Spider found that amusing. Hadn't just about everything they'd done so far been startling?

George had a telephone message as well. With so many others in the plane, he didn't want to say aloud who the message was from. Instead, he sent a group email to the other five Knights: *A message from the president of the Democratic Republic.*

When he'd called the president of the Democratic Republic from Iceland to tell him he had a plan for saving his nephew's life, he'd used his own phone, so the president knew George's phone number. The others watched as George put his phone to his ear so he could hear the message. His eyes opened wide as he listened.

When he reached the end of the recorded message, he composed another group email. His fingers were trembling as he wrote, *"Not good news. We need to meet in private ASAP."*

30

All six of them turned and marched toward the exit leading to the cargo hold. "We'll be back!" Alexis shouted over her shoulder to the others.

Cindy paused to download a few more news articles onto her phone. She'd managed to read more than twenty articles before the others showed up, but as usual, Cindy's way of thinking was that if twenty articles were good, fifty would be better.

As she was quickly downloading articles, another email message came from Denise Williams. She didn't have time to read it then, so she downloaded it for later. Then she hurried to catch up to the others.

"Let's go somewhere private," George said.

Marissa came out of the plane. "Can I come?" she asked.

"Can she?" Natalie asked the others.

"I'm fine with it," Liam said. The others nodded.

Marissa caught up with them and said, "Thanks. I understand you're all pretty close-mouthed about your plans, so don't worry. I'll keep anything you say to myself."

They headed away from the plane, toward the nearest beach. After they passed the fields and went over the first hill, Cindy could not contain her curiosity any longer. She stopped and said, "Tell us now!" she said. "Nobody's around."

They all stopped walking. George said, "There's a hitch in our plans. Cai liked the idea, a lot. So did his jailers, the refugee army. The refugees want Ja-Long out of prison alive. The president of the Democratic Republic also likes the idea. He wants his nephew alive."

"So what's the hitch?" Cindy asked.

"Ja-Long doesn't like it," George said. "He won't cooperate."

"*What?*" Alexis said. "Why not? The dude *likes* being in prison on the verge of execution?"

"I don't know why," George said. "The president said he was puzzled, too."

"I think I know why Cai wants to cooperate, but Ja-Long doesn't," Cindy said.

"Why?" George asked.

"You're a hero in the Democratic Republic," Cindy said to George. "Everyone knows you and the president have communicated privately. Plus, you just gave a very positive statement about the president, calling him peace-loving. It seems logical to me that Cai trusts us and Ja-Long doesn't."

"Also," Natalie said, "Cai is on the winning side. Ja-Long is on the losing side. Cai and his uncle and the people supporting him just won a revolution. They are in control of the new government. Ja-Long and the other refugees have been ousted. So Cai likes the way things are right now. Ja-Long doesn't. This makes Cai more eager for a deal, and Ja-Long more likely to want to make trouble."

"But Ja-Long's buddies in the refugee army like the idea," Liam pointed out.

"He hasn't been able to communicate with his buddies," Cindy said. "He is in prison so he can only talk to his jailers. It might be different if his buddies could actually talk to him and find out how he feels."

"The president wants to send Ja-Long anyway," George said. "The dude is in chains so he really has no choice. The president likes the plan and wants it to go forward. He wants his nephew alive, and he trusts us to make sure Ja-Long doesn't cause trouble."

"Oh, that's great," Alexis said. "Just what we need. A hostile, angry, uncooperative guy on our hands."

"Yeah," Liam said. "Not good."

"We got another email from Denise Williams," Cindy said. "It came just when we were leaving." She clicked open the email and read aloud:

> *It looks like your idea is going to work. You'll be able to take the two captives to your island, which will, of course, take the tensions down several notches and buy us a little time. We will dispatch a helicopter to transport Cai and Ja-Long. We'll bring them in separate helicopters. They will arrive in handcuffs. You might consider leaving them*

handcuffed. Remember that your safety is foremost.

Our plan is to leave the six men there with the helicopters as bodyguards. They will stay back and won't interfere, unless there is trouble. You won't have to worry about them. They'll come with their own tents and food.

Meanwhile, our objectives are twofold: We want to partition what is now the Democratic Republic so that the refugees will have a home. It is crucial that we find a way to house the refugees as quickly as possible. The longer they are in refugee camps, the more volatile the situation will remain.

"*Handcuffs?*" Alexis said. "No way. I vote against turning this island into a prison. I hate prisons."

"Alexis," Liam said. "Handcuffs are just common sense. One of them just helped lead a revolution. The other is a leader of a counterrevolution. They're trained soldiers. They're fighters. They're enemies. And one of them doesn't even want to come."

"Fine," Alexis said. "Then he doesn't come."

"If we have armed bodyguards," Cindy said, "I don't see why we need handcuffs."

"Excuse me," Alexis said, "but armed bodyguards are worse than handcuffs. I don't see where Denise said *armed*. She just said *bodyguards*. I say no weapons."

"I agree," Natalie said. "I don't want weapons on this island."

"We *have* weapons on this island," Spider said. "We have a hatchet, and our knives."

"We'll have to hide them away," Natalie said. "Or

get rid of them for a while."

"What do we do if one of them picks up a rock?" Spider said.

"Look," Alexis said. "I know all the arguments about how weapons don't kill people, people kill people. But if someone is going to get angry enough to reach for a weapon, I'd rather face a guy holding a rock than a hatchet or real weapon, okay?"

"The *bodyguards* have weapons!" Spider said. "Not the *prisoners*! The bodyguards have weapons in case one of the prisoners does something like pick up a rock and threaten someone."

"Number one, they are not our prisoners," Alexis said. "They are our guests. Number two, *nobody* has weapons. Number three, if nobody has a weapon, nobody can use one, and I don't want anyone using one. Any weapons, and I move to another island." She crossed her arms over her chest.

"So what do we do?" Cindy asked. "Call the whole thing off?"

They were quiet for a while, thinking.

Cindy sighed. She didn't want to see the plan unravel. On the other hand, she understood that having a trained soldier on the island who didn't want to be there might not be a good idea. And she understood not wanting armed bodyguards.

The wind picked up a bit. It was September and the days were cooling off fast. Cindy had run out without her jacket and now she felt cold. She hugged her arms to keep warm.

"I thought both of them would like the idea,"

Cindy said.

"Me, too," Natalie said. "But if either of them is so hostile that we need handcuffs or armed bodyguards, I don't think the idea will work."

"I guess we'd better go back and call Denise," Cindy said.

31

They returned to the plane to find Liam's father sitting on a cushion just outside the cargo hold. A large piece of driftwood was burning in the fireplace, giving off pungent, balsamic scent.

Liam's father stood up as they approached. "What's going on?" he asked.

Roger came from the plane.

"We need to make a phone call," Liam said. "We want to call Denise at the Nations United for Peace."

Liam and his father stood facing each other. Then Liam's father looked over the entire group. Quietly, Liam's father said, "I'd like it if we all sat down and had a talk."

The Knights of the Square Table and Marissa looked at each other, and sat down. Liam's father sat, too, and gestured for Roger to join them.

"Where's Don and the others?" Liam asked.

"Don and Tammy went to the beach. It's low tide so they're looking for food. I have no idea where Veronica is."

"What do you want to talk about?" Liam asked

him.

"I understand from interviews you've given that you vote on everything as a group before you move forward with any new plans." He paused and looked around.

"Yeah," Liam said.

"I think that means we *all* vote," Liam's father said. "That includes me, Roger, Don, Tammy, and Veronica."

Cindy looked around at the others. She had no idea how to respond, and hoped someone else knew.

"Dad," Liam said, "you and Mom make all the decisions in our house, right? You don't include me."

"That's different," he said.

"Why?" Liam asked.

"Your mother and I support the household. We're the adults. On this island, I'm just as much a contributing member of the community as you are. Roger and I brought equipment for a communication system, and we installed it. Don't we deserve the voting rights of a full citizen?"

"Does that mean you want to stay here with us?" Cindy asked.

"It means as long as I'm on this island, working as an equal member of the community, I think I should have full voting rights."

Alexis sat up straight. She looked Liam's father with a new respect. *Well*, she thought. *I guess it's no surprise that Liam's dad is smart.*

"What if you vote contrary," Alexis asked him, "just to be difficult?"

"Then you'll have to deal with that, won't you?" Liam's father turned to Cindy. "I understand you're reading political philosophy, trying to figure out how to run an ideal society."

"Right," Cindy said.

"I assume you've read Plato's *Republic*."

"Yes," Cindy said. "We all read it."

"Do you agree with Plato's ideas about the best form of government?"

"Of course not," Cindy said.

"Why?" he asked.

"Plato advocates a plain and simple aristocracy," Cindy said, "a few elite people who think they are better than the others make the decisions for everyone."

As soon as Cindy said the words, she smiled.

Check. Checkmate. He had her trapped.

Liam's father didn't smile back, but there was a spark of amusement in his eyes.

"You know what?" Alexis said. She put her fists on her hips. "I think he's right. I think everyone should vote."

"What about the bodyguards?" Spider asked. "What about Ja-Long and Cai, if they both come?"

"Everyone votes," Alexis said. "That means *everyone*. Unless someone opts out. Veronica doesn't have to if she doesn't want to."

"I'm not so sure about this," Liam said. "Working here shouldn't be enough for full voting rights. There has to be something more."

"Okay," Alexis asked. "But what?"

They all looked at each other.

"I think I know," Natalie said. She put her head onto her hands and thought hard for a few moments. When she looked up, she said, "People should have to take some sort of pledge of allegiance. You know, promise to be nice, promise to uphold our mandate of working toward world peace, that sort of thing, before they can vote."

The glint was back in Liam's father's eyes. He had a way of smiling with his eyes, while keeping the rest of his face serious. "I think I can promise to be nice." He turned to Roger. "Do you have a problem with that?"

"Not me," Roger said, holding up his hands. "And I am *entirely* in favor of world peace."

"Now you're teasing us," Cindy said.

"A little," said Liam's father. "But we're serious, too. Okay, anyone who votes must first promise to be nice, and uphold the mandate of working toward world peace. That's fair enough."

"Here's the problem with everyone voting," Cindy said. "We require all votes to be unanimous. That can work with six people, or even ten people. But what if you have twenty? Or fifty? Or a thousand? Or a million? Requiring votes to be unanimous means nothing would ever happen because you're never going to get that many people to agree."

"What's wrong with majority rule?" Roger asked.

"The problem is that the minority can get trampled," Alexis said. "I learned that the hard way."

"I'm having trouble imagining Cai and Ja-Long agreeing on anything," Liam said. "*If* we can even get them here. What do we do when nobody agrees?"

"I guess you do pretty much the same thing we do now," Alexis said. "If someone holds out, you have to figure out why they're holding out. They might have a good reason, so you have to take that into account. You can't just trample on them and say, 'You're outvoted!'"

Liam's father leaned back a little. "So if someone's holding out to be mean or just contrary, you find a way to overrule the person. But if they have a legitimate concern, you address it."

"Yes," Alexis said. "Exactly."

Cindy felt a little uncomfortable, as if they were handing over control a little too easily. For the first time she really understood Plato's objection to democracy. How could you trust a large group of people to make the right decision? She didn't trust the adults on the island to get behind some of their ideas. In particular, she didn't trust Liam's father. After all, he'd just had a meltdown when he first learned of their idea, and she could see he was toying with them now.

On the other hand, she didn't want to insist on being a member of a ruling elite. An ideal community would have to be a democracy. She understood that while democracy had its problems, it was still better than the alternatives.

"I'd like to bring up one other issue," Liam's father said. "You're keeping secrets."

"That's true," George said. "But there are some things we can't tell. For one thing, we promised we wouldn't, and we have to keep the promise. Also, there are people who trust us right now because we *are* keeping certain secrets."

"Okay, fair enough," Liam's father said. "A secret like that, you can't tell. But George, you got a phone message just now. You listened to it, and then you all marched out and had a private meeting. I think you need to include all the rest of us."

The Knights of the Square Table looked at each other. The first to speak was Alexis. "I think he's right," she said. "Does anyone disagree?"

Liam disagreed, but he wasn't about to speak up under the circumstances. The dude was *his* father. Alexis probably assumed that all parents were like hers. She was close to her parents. They talked about everything. Liam, on the other hand, hardly even knew his father. He was sure his father didn't really know him.

Evidently Liam wasn't the only one having trouble with this new development because Cindy stood up. "I need to think it over." She wandered away from the group. She went around to the other side of the plane where nobody could see her.

A few minutes later, she came back to the group and sat down. "I don't really like it," she said. "But there's something I like about inviting Cai and Ja-Long and instead of putting them in handcuffs, giving them full voting rights."

"As long as they promise to be nice," Natalie

said, "and agree to work toward world peace."

"It's a most unusual approach," Roger said. "But it has a kind of naive logic."

Cindy was about to question the naive part, but decided against it. Instead she said, "All right. I'm fine with everyone voting. I'm fine with everyone included when we get new information."

"Does everyone else agree?" George asked.

Everyone nodded and said yes.

"This," George said, "is going to get very interesting."

32

It was an hour before they had everyone assembled and explained the new rules. Everyone—even Veronica—seemed amused by the idea that anyone who wanted voting rights had to pledge to be nice and work toward world peace.

"I promise I'll try to be nice," Veronica said. "But I've decided not to take that medicine anymore, thank you very much anyway to my aunt Tammy for bringing me more. So I can't promise to live up to my promise. And in fact, I think I'd like to leave this meeting."

She stood up and walked away.

Once she was out of earshot, Alexis said to the group, "We just let her do her thing." To Roger and Liam's father, Alexis said, "She's also a klepto, so if anything of yours is missing, she's got it."

"What do you do when she takes stuff?" Roger asked.

Alexis shrugged. "We go get it back."

"All right," Liam's father said. "On with the meeting. Tell us about that phone call."

"I got a phone call from the president of the Democratic Republic," George said, "telling me Ja-Long doesn't like the idea and might not cooperate. We were about to call Denise and tell her." George looked around and said, "Any objection to me calling her now?"

Nobody had any objections, so George said, "Let's go in."

They all climbed inside the plane through the cargo hold. George dialed Denise's phone number and put her on speakerphone. Everyone listened as George told Denise what they'd learned about Ja-Long and their concerns about bringing him if he was hostile or uncooperative because they wanted no weapons or handcuffs on the island.

"I'm not actually surprised by his reaction," Denise said. "We have representatives in the Democratic Republic now. I'll have them visit Ja-Long in prison and talk to him privately to get a feel for the situation. What he tells his jailers might be a little different from what he tells us. I think he'll come around when he considers the alternatives."

"If he changes his mind," Alexis asked, "how will we know if he *really* wants to be here, or if he plans to make trouble?"

"That's a good question," Denise said. "I'll get back to you after we talk to him and try to get a sense of the situation. We certainly don't want to put anyone on that island at risk."

* * *

The Knights of the Square Table and Marissa spent the rest of the afternoon in the plane, working on their homeschool study plan. Cindy, though, was reading a book off the list just because she wanted to: B.F. Skinner's *Walden Two*. She'd learned about his book while reading about theories on how to achieve a utopia.

In the late afternoon, George received an email from Denise. She wrote:

> *Ja-Long still doesn't like the idea, but he seemed genuinely offended by the suggestion that he might commit trouble or violence on the island. He has read all about the six of you. He knows what's been in the articles and news stories. He doesn't like the public position you've taken on behalf of the Democratic Republic, but his attitude is that the six of you are young, idealistic, and misguided.*
>
> *There is nothing in our intelligence report to indicate that he might be a danger to anyone on the island. We don't see any motive or anything to be gained from violence against any of you. I can't say, though, that there is no risk. There is always risk. You'll have to decide how comfortable you feel.*

George read the email to everyone in the plane, but they didn't discuss it until everyone was assembled around the fire for a conference. Once they were all sitting down on cushions, George read the email aloud for everyone and said, "All right.

What do you all think?"

"I'm fine with it," Alexis said. "There's a risk, but everything is risky. Walking through certain neighborhoods in San Francisco is risky, too."

"Which is why we avoid those neighborhoods after dark," Liam said. "Right?"

"Right," Spider said. "But this is different! You don't go for a midnight stroll through a rough neighborhood in the interests of world peace."

"Exactly," Cindy said. "We have to remember *why* we are doing this."

"We are saving their lives," Alexis said. "Like Spider said, we're doing this in the interest of world peace. I'll take my chances."

Cindy looked around at the others. Liam's father was leaning forward, listening intently. It occurred to her that he didn't want to take control, at least after he recovered from his initial shock upon hearing their idea. He just wanted to be kept informed. She figured that was fair enough.

Liam's father caught Cindy looking at him. He said, "I'm fine with it." He turned to Roger and said, "Do you mind if we stay on this island for a while?"

"Nope," Roger said. "Not at all."

"All right," George said. "Let's take a vote. Is anyone opposed to bringing Ja-Long to the island?"

Nobody said anything.

"Good," George said. "It's decided." Then something occurred to him. "Does either of them speak English?"

"They both speak some," Cindy said. "Both

speak Mandarin as a second language."

"I speak Mandarin," Liam's father said.

"Nice," George said. "I'm glad I won't be the only one translating."

33

When the Nations United for Peace sent helicopters to each of the prisons, taking Cai aboard one of the helicopters and Ja-Long aboard the other, the event made the front pages of every major newspaper in the world and dominated all the news talk shows. Reporters came from all corners of the globe to witness both men boarding their respective helicopters.

This, after all, was no ordinary release or exchange of prisoners.

These two prisoners of war—both figureheads and leaders of their respective armies—were going to live on a remote island in the North Atlantic with a group of youngsters, the already famous Knights of the Square Table.

Predictably, some commentators said the youngsters were foolishly putting themselves in danger. Others commended their ingenuity—and bravery. Regardless of what people were saying, the plain fact was that *everyone* was talking about them. In the process, they were pondering how to best bring peace to the region.

Natalie's father posted a comment to their blog. He wrote, "Thank you very much, daughter. I'm now completely gray and losing my hair, too."

Mark, Cindy's brother, wrote, "You go, girl!"

Cindy was happy to see her brother's post. At least someone in her family got what she was trying to do.

Denise emailed George hourly updates, and he passed along her emails to everyone else. The inhabitants of the island thus knew when the helicopters were heading northwest over Europe. They knew when they stopped to refuel in Switzerland. They knew the exact time the helicopters would appear in the skies over their island.

They spent the morning working as usual. Spider and Don went fishing. A group of the others worked on building. Nobody knew where Veronica was. Liam's father went back to his usual work routine, which, with Internet access, he could do from the island almost as easily as from his office.

George spent the morning in the plane, on a laptop, answering reporters' questions. He assured everyone that they were not afraid of having two men who were sworn enemies on their island. "We are sure they are both very reasonable people who happen to have very different political views. We do not want to see either of them harmed, so we are bringing them both here."

At noon, they gathered at the fireplace not far

from the plane to prepare lunch, with the exception of Veronica, who nobody had seen all morning. When the first helicopter, the one bearing Cai, was due to arrive, they had a lunch waiting, the best the island had to offer: perfectly cooked salmon, mussels on the half shell, fragrant seaweed soup with potatoes, and for dessert, wild berries. The day, cool with a breeze, was just right for sitting around a campfire. It had rained during the night, but now the only clouds were white and cottony.

The first helicopter arrived just after noon. The helicopter was smaller and sleeker than the one Don used to ferry them back and forth to Iceland. It hovered for a moment before descending and landing on the other side of the clearing.

They all stood back to watch as the engines quieted and the blades slowed their rotations.

"Who's nervous?" Alexis asked.

"Me," Liam's father said.

"I think all of us," Liam said.

The door opened. The first to step down was a large beefy man wearing khaki pants and a shirt with buttons. The beefy man turned and helped another man out of the helicopter. The second man to emerge was also broad-shouldered, but smaller than the bodyguard. His hair was cut so short he was almost bald. His hands were cuffed behind his back.

Alexis recognized Cai immediately from the pictures of him on the news. What struck her was how young Cai was. He looked to be about twenty-two or twenty-three. She'd expected him to be older from the pictures she'd seen of him. But then, the news always showed him scowling, and now he seemed on the verge of smiling.

"A few of us should go say hello," Alexis said.

"Let's go," George said to Alexis.

George and Alexis walked briskly over to the helicopter.

"Hi!" Alexis said to Cai cheerfully. She figured everyone knew that much English. Then she said to the man standing next to him, "Please take off his handcuffs."

"You're sure?" he asked in heavily accented English.

"Yes, I'm sure," Alexis said.

The man took a key from his pocket. The key was attached to one of his belt loops by a chain. He unlocked the handcuffs.

She caught the look on Cai's face. He was surprised. Evidently nobody had told him that he would not be chained or imprisoned on the island. He stretched his arms and rubbed his wrists. To Alexis, he said—in English—"Thank you."

She smiled. "No problem! I'm Alexis." She extended her hand. He shook her hand. Then he turned to George and said something in Mandarin. George said something back.

To Alexis, George said, "He knows all our names from the articles about us."

As they walked over to the others, Cai and George talked again in Mandarin. George didn't translate for Alexis, but she didn't mind. If anyone could be trusted to say the right thing, it was George.

Meanwhile, the men who had accompanied Cai removed some folding chairs from the helicopter and sat in them. For a moment Alexis was tempted to invite them to sit around the fire, too. But when she remembered they were bodyguards, she changed her mind.

When they were all seated, George performed introductions. Then he said something else to Cai in Mandarin, and gestured toward the food.

"Yes, thank you," Cai said in English.

The others, who had already eaten, nibbled on snacks and made small talk. Cai had entirely finished his meal when they heard the sound of another helicopter approaching. Once again, only George and Alexis went to greet the new arrival.

Once the helicopter landed, the same thing happened. Another man, this one also large and beefy, descended first, then turned and helped the prisoner step down. Ja-Long was taller and leaner than Cai. Like Cai, he had an athletic build, nimble and strong. His face seemed tight and pinched.

As before, Alexis told the bodyguard to take off the handcuffs. Ja-Long, too, was surprised. Once his handcuffs were removed, they all three walked back to join the others.

"Have you two ever met?" George asked both Cai and Ja-Long. He spoke first in Mandarin, and then in English.

Cai and Ja-Long looked at each other. Cai said something in Mandarin. George translated for the others: "He says they never met."

"Even when you were at the university at the same time?" Cindy asked.

George translated, first telling Cai what Cindy had asked, and then, when Cai responded, he told Cindy, "He said no, they never met in person."

They offered Ja-Long lunch, also. While Ja-Long ate, both George and Liam's father made small talk in Mandarin with Cai and Ja-Long. Initially they translated everything for the others, but after a while, they gave up.

Cindy found that not understanding a word, just watching their expressions and listening to the inflections of their voices, gave her a pretty good sense of what was happening in the conversation. As everyone predicted, Cai seemed much more cheerful and agreeable. Ja-Long, more sullen and withdrawn. Cai looked George in the eye. Ja-Long averted his gaze.

After Ja-Long finished his meal, George called all six bodyguards over. "We're going to have a meeting," he told them.

They came, bringing their chairs.

"Okay," George said, "I'm going to say everything first in English, then I'll repeat it in Mandarin. Here's the deal. We vote on everything here. And everyone has an equal vote. For voting privileges we ask only that you promise to obey our rules." He smiled. "Fortunately, they're easy, and we have only two. First, you have to promise to be nice. Second, you have to promise to work toward our goal of world peace."

Cindy watched Ja-Long and Cai as George spoke. Both men seemed surprised and even a little amused. Cai came close to smiling. Ja-Long simply raised his brows.

"All of us vote?" one of the bodyguards asked.

"Anyone who promises to be nice and work toward world peace," George said.

Ja-Long asked a question in Mandarin. George responded, also in Mandarin.

Liam's father said, "I'll help you out here, George." To the group, he said, "Ja-Long asked whether majority rules. George told him no, it's much more interesting than that. All decisions have to be unanimous. George explained the reason."

Cindy watched as all the newcomers absorbed this. For the first time, Ja-Long and Cai glanced at each other. Even Ja-Long seemed to relax a bit.

"All right," Alexis said. "I have something to say."

George translated this. Then Alexis said, "George, tell Ja-Long that we're on his side, too."

Spider slapped his knee and said, "Hey, Alexis, there's nothing like the direct approach, right?"

"What's wrong with the direct approach?" she asked, genuinely curious.

Spider held up his hands in a gesture of surrender and said, "Nothing at all. I *like* the direct approach."

George turned to Ja-Long and translated all of this. Ja-Long said something in response.

George said, "Ja-Long says he likes the direct

approach, too. He also says, 'Then prove it. You've proved you're on the side of the military dictator. How are you going to prove you're on our side?'"

Alexis considered calling him on the use of the term 'military dictator,' which seemed to her unnecessarily provocative. Instead, she said, "Whose side do you think we were on when we brought you here? Did you *like* being in that prison?"

George and Ja-Long then launched into a conversation. Ja-Long became suddenly animated, speaking very rapidly and excitedly.

After he stopped, George said, "He says everyone is on the side of the new country because of the elections, because the dictator won by a landslide. Ja-Long says the landslide happened only because most of the refugees were not able to vote. He also says that twenty percent of the people who *could* vote voted against the dictator. He points out that twenty percent of the population is still a lot of people, and they are all angry."

"Yes!" Alexis said. "I know about getting outvoted and feeling angry." She paused so George could translate what she'd said. Then she went on: "Just because you lose an election doesn't mean it's fair. The losers can get their rights trampled on. That's why everything on our island has to be by unanimous vote."

George translated this. Ja-Long was now studying Alexis.

"I have a question," Liam said quietly. "Even if all the refugees had been allowed to vote, would they have had a majority?"

George translated his question. Ja-Long shook his head no.

"What percent would you have had?" Liam asked.

Ja-Long said, in English, "Thirty-three."

Natalie, too, had a question, but she didn't ask it. What she wondered was if his side represented only one-third of the population, how did he expect to gather an army and win a war?

34

They were startled by the distant drone of a helicopter. At first the sound was so faint they could scarcely hear it. Then, as they listened, the sound drew nearer. The helicopter was coming from the east.

Cindy's heart was suddenly racing. "Someone is coming," she said.

She could see the others, too, were alarmed. Liam's father and Roger stood up, watching the eastern sky. So did the bodyguards.

There was nothing to do but wait, and listen.

Moments later, a helicopter appeared in the distance. It seemed to be flying too fast for a landing. It approached the island, slowed down, circled several times, then flew off toward the southeast.

"I'll go see if I can find out who that was," George said. He ran to the plane and climbed in.

Cindy took out her phone to see if she could get Internet access. She couldn't. The signal was too weak for anything to load on her phone.

"I'm going with George," she said. "I just have to

know." She climbed onto the plane through the cargo hold. George was already sitting in a seat in the front row, looking at the screen of the laptop Liam's father and Roger had set up for them. On the screen was one of the major news sites.

"Do you know who that was?" Cindy asked, breathless.

"Not yet." He hit refresh. Nothing changed.

Cindy sat down next to him and looked at her phone. "We have an email from Denise!"

"There's nothing in it about the helicopters," he said. "I just checked. She wants us to do a fund-raising video to try to get money to help the refugees."

Cindy opened Denise's email and read it. Then she opened her news app and scrolled through the latest articles. The Nations United for Peace were moving swiftly: They were working on a partition—part of the country of what was now the Democratic Republic to be given to the refugees so they could have their own land. The problem was that the president of the Democratic Republic was refusing the partition. The land the refugees wanted was among the most fertile in the region and, moreover, was said to have an abundance of natural resources. Some even suspected there was oil.

"Hey!" George said. "Look at this!"

Cindy looked at his screen. There, on the blog of a news organization based in the United Kingdom, were photographs, shot from the air, of all of them sitting around the campfire. They were all staring up at the cameras. Liam's father and Roger were on their feet. Whoever was in the helicopters must have been able to transmit the photographs immediately.

"Journalists?" she asked.

"Paparazzi," he said.

"Terrific," she said. "Just terrific. Now I feel like I'm on a reality television show."

"Let's go tell the others," George said.

They went out through the cargo hold. The moment they emerged from the plane, Spider shouted, "Well? Who was it?"

"Paparazzi," George said. "Flying over, taking pictures."

George and Cindy sat back down. Cindy said, "Denise wants us to do a fund-raising blog post to get money for the refugees." She looked at George and waited for him to translate what she'd said into Mandarin. No point leaving Ja-Long and Cai out of the conversation.

Ja-Long said something. George responded.

Then Cindy said, "What did he say?"

"He said if we find housing for all the refugees, there won't be any need for a partition," George said. "He'd rather keep the refugees in camps until they were given their own land."

"Keeping people in refugee camps is not nice," Natalie said.

George translated Natalie's words, and then what Ja-Long said next: "Send food. But keep them in camps. Otherwise we'll never get our own country."

Natalie considered this. There was a brutal sort of

logic to what he was saying, even if keeping families with small children and old people in camps just for political reasons didn't seem right.

"Either way," Natalie said, "whether they stay in camps or get taken in somewhere, they need money, right? Lots of it. I think we should do a video instead of a blog post. We can film George asking everyone for money and post that on our blog. Maybe it will go viral."

"Everything we do goes viral," George said. "I can't see where asking for money would hurt."

So much of this conversation had been in English that Liam's father waved for attention, and then repeated what had been said in Mandarin for Ja-Long and Cai.

Cai said something in Mandarin.

George translated. "Cai says he votes against making a video."

Everyone turned to look at Cai. He raised his chin and, in English, said, "I say no."

Natalie opened her mouth to speak, but stopped. She had been about to tell him that votes based in nothing but meanness were not allowed. Then she thought of another, more immediate problem.

"If you want to vote," she told him, "you have to promise to be nice and work in the interest of world peace."

George translated this for Cai. He listened, and then blinked, surprised.

Cai said something in Mandarin. George translated: "He says he promises to be nice and work toward world peace. He also votes against a fund-raising video."

"How is that not mean?" Natalie asked.

"It is not mean," Cai said in English. Then he spoke rapid Mandarin. Ja-Long sat up straighter, obviously not liking whatever Cai had said.

George translated: "Cai said the money is not used for food or shelter. He said the rebels use it for guns and raising an army to fight them."

"Hey," Alexis said. "No words like 'rebel' or 'dictator.' Nice words only, please."

Liam's father translated this for Cai and Ja-Long. Cai said, "No video. I vote no."

35

Natalie was sitting very still, thinking. It wasn't hard to understand why Cai didn't want a fund-raising video. The harder part was to understand why Ja-Long wanted a war he probably wouldn't win. It took several minutes before she made the connection: He might not win the war on the battlefield, but with families homeless and in refugee camps, he could win the public relations battle.

Natalie didn't realize she was staring at Ja-Long, until he glanced up. Their eyes met. Embarrassed to be caught staring, she looked down at her hands.

Someone needed to do something. Sitting here looking at each other simply wouldn't do. She stood up, went to the cargo hold, and came back with a chess set.

"Who wants to play?" she asked.

In English, Ja-Long said, "I will play." He pointed to Natalie and said something in Mandarin.

"He wants to play against you," George told Natalie.

She shrugged. "Okay."

Don switched places with Ja-Long so that Ja-Long could sit next to Natalie. Natalie put the board down between them and began setting up the pieces. She gave Ja-Long white, which would give him a slight advantage.

Once the pieces were set up, Ja-Long made his move. He pushed his king's pawn forward two spaces.

Natalie glanced at Liam, and she saw that he was thinking the same thing: Was Ja-Long really, really good, or had he accidentally settled on one of the most sophisticated and complex openings known in chess?

She knew what to do. She moved her white bishop's pawn two spaces. The quickness of her move seemed to startle Ja-Long. She felt him watching her, but kept her eyes on the chessboard. She wanted to beat him. If he was as good as this opening suggested, she would need to concentrate.

Ten moves later, it was clear Ja-Long knew what he was doing. Natalie was playing an aggressive game, not because she necessarily wanted to, but because he gave her no choice. He positioned himself quickly and confidently to take control of the center of the board. One weak move on her part, and he'd have complete dominance over the key squares.

"He's a hustler," Spider said. "The dude's pretty good."

Liam agreed. He was watching the board as intensely as Natalie and Ja-Long. *Come on, Natalie, he urged silently.*

Natalie was so still and looked at the board for so long that anyone watching would have thought she was in a trance. Liam knew better, though. He had seen her play chess too many times. He knew she was doing her intuition thing. He also knew her next move would be brilliant.

She moved a pawn. Liam blinked, surprised and disappointed. It was a timid move in a game with an aggressive player—a game in which she couldn't afford to be timid. In moving that pawn, she'd opened up her queen. It was almost as if she was inviting an attack.

It was now Ja-Long's move. Ja-Long hesitated a long time, then castled. What surprised Liam was that Ja-Long took so long to decide when it was such a strong move. He was now sitting in one of the most secure positions possible in chess: His king was guarded by three pawns, with the knight two squares in front, and of course, the castle by the king's side.

For her next turn, Natalie moved a little too quickly. She moved her bishop, then pulled back both of her hands and placed them in her lap in a subtle gesture of regret.

Now Liam understood what Natalie was doing. He wanted to smile, but he kept his face completely impassive.

Ja-Long, who usually thought carefully about each move, took the bait. He moved his knight to capture her bishop.

She held very still. It was as if she were holding her breath. She took his knight with her queen, which exposed her king. Ja-Long was confident now. He moved a castle in position to attack the pawn guarding her king.

Now it was Natalie's move.

She moved her queen three squares forward. Then came the moment that always made her uneasy. But she lifted her chin and looked Ja-Long directly in the eye when she said, "Checkmate."

Ja-Long sat up straighter. He looked down at the board and blinked. His mouth opened, but he didn't say anything. She'd done it. His king was neatly trapped.

Natalie clasped her hands together and held them near her chin. After that, both Ja-Long and Natalie sat very still. Ja-Long was looking at the board so intently that Liam knew he was thinking back over the past half dozen moves to find his mistake.

At last, Ja-Long said something in Mandarin.

"What did he say?" Natalie asked George.

"He says you pretended to make a mistake when you moved the bishop, but you knew what you were doing. You sacrificed the bishop to open up his king, then distracted him by tricking him into attacking you. He says you bluffed him."

"I did," Natalie said quietly. "Please apologize for me. Tell him he's a good player, so bluffing him was the only way I could win."

That was when Liam noticed that his father was looking at Natalie with something like awe. *See, Dad,* he wanted to say—although precisely why he wanted to say that wasn't clear to him. Then his father glanced at him, and they looked at each other for a long moment.

Liam's father must have seen *See, Dad*, in Liam's eyes, because quietly he said to Liam, "I never doubted that the members of this team can play a good game of chess."

Natalie cleared her throat. What she did next took Liam completely by surprise. She turned to Cai, smiled sweetly, and asked, "Would you like to play?"

Firmly, Cai shook his head no.

"I'll let you start," Natalie said.

Cai evidently understood this because he responded by speaking Mandarin. When he finished, George said, "He said if he *did* play, he wouldn't care which color he played. He'd even play Alexis. But he has no intention of playing."

Obviously Cai knew from articles about them that Alexis was the strongest player on the team, which meant they both probably knew Natalie was weakest.

In English, Ja-Long said, "I will play again. I will play Natalie."

Liam pointed to Alexis and said, "This time play against Alexis. Or George."

"Yeah," Alexis said to Ja-Long. "Play one of us. We don't bluff our way out of tight corners."

"They don't," Natalie said. "Especially Alexis. If she ever does get boxed in, which isn't often, she *fights* her way out."

Ja-Long spoke again in Mandarin. When he finished, George said to Natalie, "Ja-Long wants to play against you again. He says he underestimated you. He also says you're a very gracious winner."

Natalie looked at Ja-Long and said, "I think next you should play Alexis."

Ja-Long smiled and spoke again.

"Well, now what did he say?" Natalie asked George.

"He says he wants to play *you*."

Natalie understood why. She beat him by bluffing him, but it was a tactic that rarely worked twice. "I think I'll quit while I'm ahead," she said.

Ja-Long said something else.

When he finished, George said to Natalie, "He wants to know if you understand that chess is a game of war, and a brutal one. We sacrifice our pawns so the king can live. He says it is interesting that a group of peace-loving youngsters plays a war game."

"It *feels* like a game of war," Natalie said. "If one player doesn't resign, it's like a fight to the death. But it isn't really. You win by your brains and not your bombs or guns. And that's a smarter way to win."

That was when George noticed that Cindy hadn't said a word. He looked at her. She was very still and alert, listening to everything.

He wondered what she was thinking.

36

Cindy was thinking that you could learn so much about people by watching them play chess.

Suddenly Spider sprang to his feet. "Sorry, folks, but I can't sit this long. My legs just won't do it. I need to go climb a big rock. Does anyone mind?"

He looked around at everyone. Nobody objected, so he said, "Anyone want to come?"

Alexis wanted to go, badly. Seeing the look on Alexis's face, Spider said, "Come on, Alexis. We can get some mussels for snacks."

"All right," she said, rising. "If nobody minds."

Everyone shook their heads to show they didn't mind. Alexis and Spider walked off together.

Liam, watching them walk off, had a hard time hiding his pleasure. Since returning to the island, he'd been watching Spider and Alexis for signs that the romance between them was progressing. He had even amused himself by thinking up ways to hurry things along. His favorite idea—completely impractical but fun to imagine—was to find a way to trap them together somewhere for a few days.

He looked around. Cindy, too, was watching them walk away with a hint of a smile on her face. He remembered his reaction when she'd suggested that Alexis would be a better match for Spider. He'd been doubtful. Now he could see she was right.

* * *

They prepared supper from the crates of food Liam's father had brought.

George went into the plane to answer email and respond to reporters. When he'd finished, he and Cindy sat in the pilot and copilot's seats, their favorite places to sit and read. They weren't reading, though. They held their books and pretended to read while Cindy shared her observation with George: Ja-Long was ruthless and wanted to win at any cost.

They couldn't meet anymore as a group without Liam's father insisting on being part of the meeting—which made things a little awkward. Sometimes you just didn't want to share every thought or idea you had with everyone. But Natalie, who came into the plane to get a fresh change of clothes, could see Cindy and George were talking about something. She joined them, and added her own observations about Cai and Ja-Long.

"Cai is more timid," Natalie said, "and he cares more about what people think of him. He didn't want to play because he didn't think he could win. He would have rather played Alexis than me because if you lose to the strongest player it doesn't look as bad as losing to the weakest player."

Later, while gathering firewood, George had the chance to tell the others what Natalie and Cindy thought about Cai and Ja-Long.

The bodyguards adjusted their chairs so they reclined slightly, and slept in their chairs. The adults—Don, Veronica, Tammy, Liam's father, and Roger—slept in the plane. The girls hung a tarp over the entrance to the cargo hold and slept inside. The guys, including Ja-Long and Cai, slept in sleeping bags outside, within sight of the bodyguards.

* * *

Spider woke the next morning to the sound of a helicopter. He didn't pay much attention. He assumed one of those paparazzi helicopters was flying overhead. The sound of engines faded away.

He sat up and looked around. Ja-Long's sleeping bag was empty. Ja-Long was nowhere in sight. He figured Ja-Long had stepped into the bushes to do some early morning business. He waited, but Ja-Long didn't return. He got out of his sleeping bag—he was fully dressed in athletic clothing, which was what they all used for pajamas—and walked around, looking for Ja-Long.

He didn't see him. One of the bodyguards opened his eyes.

"I don't see Ja-Long," Spider said.

The bodyguard bolted to his feet. Two other bodyguards also woke up and were instantly on their feet.

They walked in a large circle around the plane,

looking for him. When they concluded that he wasn't in the vicinity, one of the bodyguards said to Spider, "Maybe you should call to the people in the plane."

Spider walked over to the plane. He raised his voice and said, "Hey, everyone! I hate to do this, but everyone needs to wake up."

Alexis pushed aside the tarp. "What's the matter?"

"Ja-Long isn't here," Spider said.

"I heard a helicopter," Alexis said.

"I heard that helicopter, too," said one of the bodyguards. "The helicopter couldn't have him. It didn't land. It circled the island and left."

"Could they have dropped a ladder?" Liam's father asked.

"It's possible," said the bodyguard, "but not very likely."

A few of them spread out, calling to Ja-Long. There was no answer.

"We need to find him," said one of the bodyguards.

They had a large tub of drinking water from the evening before, so breakfast was a cup of water and a protein bar from the box Liam's father opened.

They divided into three groups, each group heading a different direction, with Tammy remaining at the plane as a contact person.

George's group consisted of himself, Spider, Cai, one of the bodyguards, Alexis, and Cindy. His group set off immediately, heading southward, to a part of the island they hadn't explored much because of the steep cliffs at the beach.

They hadn't gone far when Veronica came running toward them, pointing. She was breathing so hard it took several moments before she could speak.

"One of the guys is over there," she said. "I heard him. He sounded like he was far away down a hill. He shouted something in Chinese."

"Is he hurt?" Spider asked.

"I don't know," Veronica said.

"Do you want to come with us and show us?" Alexis asked Veronica.

"I can't." She was still so out of breath that speaking was difficult. "I ran all the way back here. I can't walk anymore. Just walk that direction," she said, pointing southward. "It's a long way. Just keep going."

"Thanks, Veronica," George said. "The rest of us better go."

"Tammy is by the plane," Alexis told her.

As the group set off, George noticed that Cai stayed very close to him, almost like a shadow. At first it worried him, and then he assumed that Cai just wanted to be near the only other person in the group who would understand him if he talked. The bodyguard evidently noticed, too, because he stayed close to both of them.

They walked at least a half mile, probably farther, occasionally shouting out to Ja-Long and stopping to listen for a response. They must have been walking up a hill, but the slope was so gradual nobody noticed. Suddenly Alexis stopped and said, "Look!

We're really high!" She pointed into the distance, where you could see the ocean.

That was when they heard Ja-Long shout.

"He's calling for help," George said. He took a few steps and said, "He's down there!"

George took another step. Either he slipped on a rock, or the ground at the edge of the precipice slid out from under him. He lost his balance and fell. Cai shouted something and reached for George and grabbed his arm, trying to pull him back up. That was when they both slid down.

"Everyone stand back!" the bodyguard shouted.

They heard the sound of rocks tumbling down the slope. George cried out in pain. From his voice it was clear he was sliding all the way down.

Spider edged forward to look. Immediately he saw the problem. The drop-off was entirely hidden by a row of shrubs.

"Stay back!" the bodyguard ordered.

"I know what I'm doing," Spider said.

The bodyguard leaned to reach for Spider, but Alexis stopped him. "He's a rock climber," she said. "He really does know what he's doing."

Spider stepped forward carefully, testing the ground before he put his weight down. "Everyone else get back!" Spider said. "I don't want too much weight on this cliff. I have to see where they are."

They all took several steps backward, watching as Spider tested the ground carefully with each step. At last, he bent forward to look.

"They're all three down there," Spider said. "On a

stretch of beach between two piles of rock." Then, he shouted down, "Are you okay?"

Cai yelled something back, but of course Spider didn't understand. Then George shouted, "We're okay! I'm the only one hurt!"

"Where are you hurt?" Spider shouted.

"My wrist! My ankle! And everything else!"

"Oh, this is just great," Alexis said. "Now Cai and Ja-Long have the perfect chance to try to kill each other—with George there."

"If anyone should be there with them," Cindy said, "it's George. George can't out-fight anyone, but he can out-*talk* anyone."

Spider wasn't paying attention. He was leaning over, sizing up the hill. "There is no way we can pull them up. There is too much danger of rocks falling on them. They're going to have to get into the water and go around those boulders. It looks like the easier way is that way." Spider pointed northward.

"The water is freezing!" Alexis said.

"The water is still about six feet back," Spider said. "I'll run back to the plane. We need flotation cushions and rope. Everyone else, go down to that stretch of beach and start a fire so we can warm them up when we get them out of there. You can probably get to the beach around that way." He pointed.

"I'll go back with you," Alexis said.

Spider leaned over and shouted, "Don't try to climb out of there! It's too steep on the other side! We'll make a raft and come get you!"

"Okay," George shouted back.

Spider and Alexis took off running back to the plane.

37

George, Ja-Long, and Cai sat together on the beach, facing the water. George was in pain—his ankle hurt, his wrist hurt, and he felt a piercing pain in his side. It amazed him that Cai went down the slope without injury.

"You just rolled," George said to Cai.

"That way you don't break bones," Cai said. "You tried to break your fall, and probably broke your wrist."

Talking to Ja-Long and Cai was easier for George when he didn't have to worry about translating everything into English. "Yeah," he said. "It hurts." At first the pain had been searing, but when he held still, it receded somewhat.

"Thanks for trying to grab me," George said to Cai.

George wanted to know why Ja-Long had wandered away like that, but he had no intention of asking. Both men were sitting calmly, or as calmly as you can after tumbling down a steep slope. George looked back up and tried to guess how many feet they'd rolled down, but from where they sat, it was hard to tell.

Ja-Long gazed upward, too, and said, "That was quite a fall."

George looked at Ja-Long, then at Cai. He understood he had an amazing opportunity—and he didn't want to waste it. There was only so much you could say in front of an audience. Now it was just the three of them.

George held still until the pain receded a bit. Then he said, "I have a proposal. Let's take the whole world by surprise. Let's come off of this beach with a new resolution. You two shake hands. Cai, you agree to the partition. Ja-Long, you stop fighting."

George was sitting between them, so all he could do was look from one to the other. He would have liked to be able to see them both at once.

"And then you, George Cheung, emerge as the wonder boy who brought peace," Cai said.

"Nope," George said. "I do not want to be the wonder boy. I want no credit. I think the credit should go to Cai." *Cai cares about appearances*, Natalie had said.

"Why him?" Ja-Long demanded. "Why should *he* get credit?"

"Because he's giving up the most," George said. "You're getting the most. He's sitting in the winner's seat right now. So we come off this beach with the resolution that Cai had a change of heart. Cai gets all the credit. The two of us, me and Ja-Long, will be surprised and grateful." George turned to Cai. "What do you say to that?"

"Even if I agree, what good will that do?" Cai asked. "It's not like I can tell my uncle what to do."

"You make a public statement and then we call him privately and ask him to do it."

"He doesn't want to give up all that land," Cai said.

"He doesn't have to give it all up," George said. "He just sits at the negotiating table and everyone agrees on where to draw the new boundaries. What's the alternative? Both of you staying here on this island forever? Getting news reports and more fighting and killing?"

This was met with silence. George said to Cai, "You'll be the hero. The peace-loving, generous-spirited hero who doesn't want to see poor refugees meet their death."

"So I have a change of heart, and then what?" Cai asked.

"Then Ja-Long is grateful and calls on the army to disband," George said. "I make a video asking for food to be sent to the refugees and supplies so they can build homes."

Ja-Long wants to win at any cost, Cindy had said.

George looked at Ja-Long and said, "Cai looks like a hero, but you come out the winner. You can go home and say that you got everything you wanted."

That was when George realized Cai and Ja-Long were looking at each other. They seemed to be watching each other's eyes.

* * *

When Spider and Alexis arrived back at the plane, Tammy said, "You found him, right?"

"Yup," Alexis said. "Just where Veronica said he was. He went over a cliff and he's trapped on a stretch of beach. George and Cai also slid down. Cai tried to grab him, then they both slid down."

Meanwhile, Spider grabbed a backpack and stuffed it with warm clothing and blankets. "We need flotation cushions and rope. We have to bring them back in the water."

Alexis went into the plane for flotation cushions. Veronica got the rope from a corner of the cargo hold where they kept tools and supplies.

Once they had everything they needed, Spider and Alexis then ran back to the beach where—they hoped—the others had a fire started.

They found quite a crowd at the beach, along with a small fire. His group had met up with the group consisting of Natalie, Marissa, Roger, and two of the bodyguards.

When they reached the others, they dropped the stuff they'd been carrying. Spider set right to work, zipping the cushions together to make a raft. Several others helped him. Next they tied the rope to one of the handles. Spider tested the knot to make sure it would hold.

"Now what are you going to do?" Natalie asked Spider.

"I'm going over there to get them," Spider said.

"I'll go, too," one of the bodyguards said.

Spider turned and looked at the bodyguard. He was large, and obviously strong. "I think it will be too much weight on the raft," Spider said.

"I think he's right," Roger said. "Plus he's bringing three people back."

"I don't know about him going alone," the bodyguard said.

"Look," Spider said, "when I tug on the rope, pull me back. If I pull hard, over and over, it means I ran into a problem and someone's gotta come get me. Okay?"

"All right," the bodyguard said.

Spider waded into the water, and pulled himself onto the raft. He didn't have anything to paddle with, so he kept one leg in the water, and pushed off against the rocks. The water was cold and biting. Soon his leg felt frozen. The cold caused him to breathe hard.

He worked the raft around the first of the boulders. Each breaking wave pushed him against the boulders. He pushed back off with either a hand or a foot, whichever of them could manage. With each push he propelled himself forward a few inches.

Once in a while a wave pulled him so far out to sea all he could do was wait for the next wave to carry him back.

Soon his hands grew raw, and sore, and very cold. His wet leg was so cold it felt like it had turned to solid ice. He didn't know if it had started to drizzle, or if he was just feeling the spray from the waves.

At last, he made it around the largest boulder.

Seeing him, Cai and Ja-Long stood up, and both helped George walk by putting one of George's arms over each of their shoulders.

George climbed onto the raft with Spider. Cai and Ja-Long held on, but kept their legs in the water. Once they were ready, Spider jerked on the rope and shouted, "Pull us back!"

He felt the tugging as the others pulled the rope.

Getting back was much easier. All they had to do was keep pushing off from the boulders. It couldn't have taken longer than four or five minutes for them to reach the other side, but Spider was so cold it felt like hours.

As soon as they could, they all let go of the raft and waded back to the shore, with George leaning on both Cai and Ja-Long.

The others were waiting with towels and warm clothing. "I want to get into that hot spring," Spider said. "As soon as I thaw out enough to walk!"

Spider, Ja-Long, and Cai sat as close to the fire as they could, rubbing their hands together to warm them. The others sat nearby.

Just then, they heard the faraway rumble of a helicopter. Nobody moved. There wasn't much to do but look up into the sky to see if the helicopter might land. It didn't. It circled all the way around the island.

When it was almost directly overhead, Natalie said, "Come on, everyone! Smile and wave! We're going to be on the news!"

They all watched as the helicopters circled once more over the island, and flew off in the direction of

Iceland.

They sat silently until George, Cai, and Ja-Long stopped shivering and relaxed. Alexis put more wood on the fire.

"As soon as George dries off and warms up," Don said, "I'll take him to Iceland and a hospital. George, can you ask if Cai or Ja-Long needs to see a doctor?"

Both said they were fine and didn't need a doctor.

The sound of the ocean was calming. Clouds were rolling in and a slight breeze was blowing. For several minutes, they sat in silence.

Then Cai said something in Mandarin.

Liam's father said, "I'll translate. He says he has an announcement."

Cai began speaking. Liam's father listened, astonished. When Cai finished talking, Liam's father held still, as if in disbelief. Then he said, "Cai says he had a change of heart. He will call on his uncle and the people of the new Democratic Republic and ask for a partition. He wants to see the conflict end."

Next, Ja-Long said something in Mandarin. When he finished speaking, Liam's father translated. "Ja-Long says he is grateful, and in return, he promises to ask the new army to stop fighting so the region can have peace."

Everyone was silent.

At last, Liam's father turned to George. "How did you do it?"

"I did nothing," George said, holding up his hands. "I swear. I had no idea either of them were going to say anything like this!"

The other five Knights of the Square Table knew George was lying. They knew George well enough so they could tell: Whenever he spoke just a little too confidently and just a little too earnestly, and when he sounded so believable you thought nobody could doubt him, it meant he was lying.

While the other adults obviously believed him, Liam could see that his father was doubtful.

* * *

Later that afternoon, Spider called, "Hey, everyone! Come look! George is being interviewed right now in Iceland! You can see it live!"

Anyone within earshot of the plane hurried to see.

The headlines across the screen declared, "In under 48 Hours, the Wonder Kids Succeed."

George was on the screen. A young dark-haired woman was holding a microphone for him to speak into. His arm was in a sling.

"We did nothing," George said. "First Cai and then Ja-Long had a change of heart."

The woman holding the microphone asked, "Can you give us some idea how it came about? What caused this change of heart?"

"I think it happened because of the accident," George said. "First Ja-Long slipped and went down the slope. I was about to fall, when Cai tried to grab me, but then we both slipped down."

"But how did tumbling down a slope cause this

change of heart?" she asked.

"I can only guess," George said earnestly. "It seems to me going over a cliff can really shake a person up. You can get a whole new perspective on problems."

"But what part did *you* play in this?"

"None at all, other than being a little clumsy. As my friends like to say, I'm not the most coordinated guy on the planet. I'm very grateful to Cai for trying to stop me from falling over. He could have stepped back and saved himself a few bruises. Instead he tried to save me."

"I cannot believe you take no credit for this change of heart," she said.

"I would *love* to take credit if I could," George said. "Trust me. I'm not a modest sort of guy." He flashed his most appealing smile. "But I did nothing. All the credit goes to Cai, an extremely reasonable man. In fact, I think that region will be in good hands under *both* their leadership."

"What about the others in your group? Did any of them do anything to help bring this about?"

"Oh, yes," George said, "as a matter of fact. Cindy came up with the idea of inviting both men to our island, to be our guests. She wanted to diffuse the tense situation in the region and make sure neither man was harmed in any way."

"What are your plans now?"

"We have some high school coursework to catch up on," George said. "And whatever projects come our way next."

Just then, Cindy's telephone buzzed. She pulled it out of her pocket and looked. She'd received an email from her mother. "Congratulations, Cindy," her mother wrote.

"Thanks, Mom," she wrote back.

38

Liam took his guitar and went to sit on a large flat rock near the fields. He'd been working on a new song. He strummed the opening chords, and sang:

Just imagine harmony,
An island in the wide blue sea.
A dream of peace, a place to be.

Just imagine there's a girl,
Whose very shoulders bear the world,
A visionary who can see,
A world of peace for you and me.
Imagine there's a boy who knows,
Where she leads him, he will go.

Imagine another kind of life:
Melody harmonized from strife.
Just imagine amity.
If you imagine, it will be.

He was happy with the lyrics, but the melody and

mood of the music still were not right. He wanted the music to be celebratory and joyful, but also soothing with a touch of mystery. He planned to play the song for Natalie, once it was finished.

"That's good, Liam," came his father's voice. He turned to find his father standing just behind him.

"Dad!" Liam said, surprised.

Liam moved to make room for his father on the boulder.

His father sat down and said, "I've never heard that song."

"That's because I wrote it. I'm still working on it."

"Nice," his father said. "Very nice. Will you play it once more?"

Liam played it again. He experimented a bit with the melody, and thought this time he achieved more mystery and depth.

When he finished playing, he father asked, "So, how did George do it?"

"I don't know exactly," Liam said. "I only know generally."

"Tell me generally."

"He knew what to say to get Cai and Ja-Long to agree."

"I can guess that much. How did he know?"

"Cindy says chess is a window into a person's soul. After the chess game, Cindy and Natalie felt like they had Cai and Ja-Long sized up."

"Cai didn't play chess," Liam's father said.

"They guessed why he didn't want to play, and

that told them a lot about him."

"Why didn't he want to play?"

"Dad, you can't ask me to tell you any more. Cai and Ja-Long trust George because they know George won't talk. And George *didn't* talk. But if we put it together and figure out exactly what George said and why, that's the same as George telling."

His father looked off in the distance. Liam strummed a few more chords. He realized that it felt good to be sitting there, talking to his father.

"It doesn't make any sense," his father said. "People don't just switch positions like that. This sort of thing doesn't happen."

Liam felt confused. Hadn't his father just witnessed two people changing their positions?

But it just did, Liam almost said. Instead, he said, "Why not?"

"I don't know why not. I know that peacekeeping groups can try for years to make something like that happen, and they don't succeed."

"But people change their minds all the time. Why is it so surprising for people to change their minds when they see they're on a crash course? Besides, it's not like all the problems are over. It just means now they're talking."

"If it's really this easy," Liam's father said, "if people can be sensible and change direction when they see they're on a crash course, why are there wars?"

"That's what Cindy and the others wondered."

"Not you?" his father asked.

"To tell the truth, I was skeptical. I went along when the others wanted to start solving all the major problems in the world, but I thought Cindy was nuts. I didn't really think we could accomplish much."

"Now you do?"

"Yeah. Maybe Don was right. Maybe kids can do things that adults can't do. Marissa told Natalie that the situation with the nuclear bombs bothered her when she first learned about it, and then she just got used to it. Kids aren't *used* to anything yet."

"I'll give you that. A kid sees things fresh. I would have wanted to do something like this when I was your age."

"I'll bet a lot of people would," Liam said.

His father sighed. "After this, you kids are going to have more offers coming your way. But why can't you do this from home? Why do you have to be on an island off the coast of Iceland? I understand, in this case, it was helpful to have an island to get those men out of the conflict. But there's really no need to stay here, is there?"

"There is," Liam said. "At least for a while."

"Why?"

Because this island is like a temple, Liam considered saying. *Or the mountaintop where you find wisdom.*

He decided against a poetic answer and dug deeper for the reason. "We had a hard time going back to our regular lives after being here," he said. "After doing things our way for a while, it was frustrating to go home and see big problems but not be able to fix them when solutions seemed obvious."

Liam looked toward the hills, which seemed as untouched and remote as when they'd first arrived. He still remembered his first impression of the island when there was snow on the ground and the air was so crisp and clean, and the gold specks glittered in the hills. He also remembered that morning looking into the tide pool with Alexis and Spider and thinking he could stay forever. He didn't really want to stay forever. But he wasn't ready yet to go.

"But why *here*?" his father asked. "Why can't you fix the problems from home?"

"Being here gives us a better view of the world. We can't get used to the way things are because we're not in them."

Liam strummed the opening chords to his new song again. He thought about Cai and Ja-Long, and Cindy and George, and it occurred to him that he should write a song called "Dear World."

Dear World,

See? It *can* be done.

Knights of the Square Table 3 is now available:

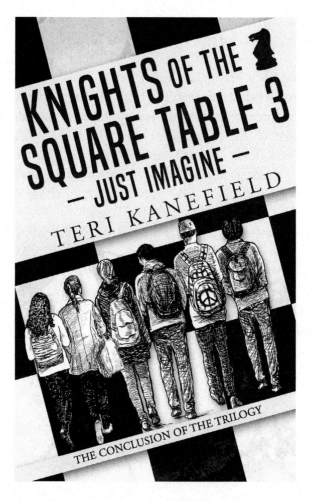

Six teenagers determined to bring about global nuclear disarmament run into a problem: It may not be possible. After all they've been through and done, will they now have to accept defeat?

ABOUT THE AUTHOR

Teri writes novels, short stories, essays, stories for children, and nonfiction for both children and adults.

Her recent books for young readers include *The Girl from the Tar Paper School*, which won the 2015 Jane Addams Book Award and National Council for Social Studies Carter G. Woodson Middle Level Book Award. Her first novel, *Rivka's Way*, was a Sydney Taylor Awards Notable Book.

Her stories have appeared in publications as diverse as *Education Week*, *Scope Magazine*, *The Iowa Review*, *The American Literary Review*, and *Cricket Magazine*.

Teri lives with her family in California near the beach.

CPSIA information can be obtained
at www.ICGtesting.com
Printed in the USA
LVOW01s1031100716

495761LV00017B/831/P